"How does lying look?"

What was the matter with her? She sounded like a fool, and she didn't seem to be able to stop it. "I mean to you. How can you tell?"

"Lack of eye contact." He moved closer. "A tense, closed expression, halting speech, hesitation."

He certainly didn't look tense. He looked powerful, in control and way too sexy.

"Take now," he said, leaning ever so slightly forward. "Your expression is open. You're not nervous. It's like you're inviting me in. Like you want me to see your innermost thoughts," he continued.

She definitely didn't want that.

"Like you're thinking of physical contact…" He brushed her fingers, gently holding the tips of hers with the tips of his. He drew in a deep breath. "Wouldn't be a bad thing."

She felt a warmth rise over her wrist, up the inside of her arm and through to her chest. She didn't want him to let go.

One Baby,
Two Secrets

BARBARA
DUNLOP

First published in Great Britain 2016
By Mills & Boon, an imprint of HarperCollins*Publishers*
1 London Bridge Street, London, SE1 9GF

Large Print edition 2017

© 2017 Barbara Dunlop

ISBN: 978-0-263-07201-3

Printed and bound in Great Britain
by CPI Antony Rowe, Chippenham, Wiltshire

To my husband.

One

Stale cigarette smoke warred with sharp memories as Kate Dunhern stood in the doorway of her mother's tattered third-floor walk-up in south central Los Angeles.

"Darling," her mother Chloe cried, pulling her into a bony embrace.

Chloe's hair was cut spiky short, her tank top crisp with colored sequins, and the scent of Vendi Dark Mist wafted in an invisible cloud around her. The floor seemed to shift momentarily, and Kate was transported back to her childhood.

"I didn't think you'd come," Chloe singsonged, rocking Kate back and forth in her arms.

"Of course I came," Kate said, firming her stance and waiting for the embrace to end.

"It's been terrible on us all," Chloe said with a sniff, finally pulling back and giving Kate space to breathe.

"I can't believe she's gone." An image of her sister, Francie, formed in Kate's mind.

She saw Francie as a teenager, grinning as they dug into a bowl of ice cream with colored sprinkles. The memory was good. But it was followed swiftly by the memory of Francie shouting that she hated Chloe before storming out of the apartment and slamming the door.

Not that Kate blamed Francie for bailing. Chloe had never been a candidate for mother of the year.

She had loved her daughters when the mood struck her and ignored them when it didn't. She'd criticized them when she was in a bad mood, which was most of the time. She claimed they had cramped her style, ruined her figure and kept her home with their snotty-nosed whining when she'd rather be out with an eligible man. In Chloe's mind, the only thing between her and happily ever after with some handsome, wealthy Prince Charming had been the anchor of Kate and Francie.

Kate had followed Francie's lead, leaving for Seattle with her best friend, Nadia Ivanova, as soon as they'd graduated high school. She and Nadia had supported each other through teachers' college, and she'd never looked back, at least not until now. Not until Francie had been killed in a car accident.

"She was drinking, you know," Chloe said, closing the apartment door and crossing the worn braided rug on high heels.

"I read the news article." Kate was the last person to defend Francie's actions, but she bristled at the critical tone in her mother's voice.

Chloe lifted a glass of orange juice from the small, chipped dining table. "She should have known better."

Even if ice cubes hadn't clinked against the glass as she drank, Kate would have guessed the juice was laced with vodka.

Because of the great example you set for us? The sarcastic question rang silent in Kate's mind.

"When is her service?" she asked instead.

Chloe waved a dismissive hand. "She didn't want a service."

"It doesn't have to be big or fancy," Kate said.

They were anything but a close-knit family, but they were Francie's only family. They needed to say goodbye.

"The body was already cremated."

"What? When?" Kate's knees went unexpectedly weak, the finality of her sister's death suddenly hitting home.

She was never going to see Francie again. Visions of her sister bloomed in earnest now, at eight years old, reading *The Jolly Green Frog* to Kate on their shared mattress in the back bedroom, the time she'd tried to bake peanut butter cookies and nearly lit the kitchen on fire, the two of them on the floor in front of the television, watching a thoroughly inappropriate late-night crime drama with Chloe passed out on the sofa.

Kate moved now to touch that sofa, that same old burgundy brocade sofa. She lowered herself to the saggy cushion.

"Why would you do that?" she asked her mother, her throat tight.

"It wasn't me," Chloe said.

"The hospital decided to cremate her?"

Had Chloe pleaded poverty? Was cremation the default decision for patients who died without the means to pay for a funeral? Chloe should have come to Kate. Kate didn't have a lot of money, but she could have buried her own sister.

"Quentin decided to cremate her. He said it was what she wanted. He can afford anything he wants without blinking an eye, so I expect he was telling the truth." Chloe took a large swallow of the orange juice drink.

"Quentin?" Kate prompted.

"Francie's boyfriend, Annabelle's father."

"Who is Annabelle?"

Chloe blinked at Kate for a moment. "Francie's baby."

Kate was glad to be sitting down. "Francie..." Her voice failed her before she could finish the sentence. She cleared her throat and tried again. "Francie has a baby?"

"You didn't know?"

"How would I know?" Kate hadn't spoken to either her mother or her sister in nearly seven years. "Is the baby all right? Where is she?" Kate found herself glancing around the apartment, wondering if her niece might be sleeping in the bedroom.

Chloe obviously guessed the direction of Kate's thoughts and drew back in what looked like alarm. "She's not here. She's where she belongs, with her father, Quentin Roo."

As he had for nearly a month now, Brody Calder pretended to be amused by Quentin Roo's crude, misogynistic remarks. The man's current target was swimsuit model Vera Redmond, who was clad in a clingy black sheath of a minidress, sipping a crimson martini across the crowded pool deck of Quentin's Hollywood Hills mansion.

"Could bounce a quarter off it," Quentin stated with a low, meaningful chuckle.

"I have," said Rex Markel, causing Quentin to laugh harder.

Brody smiled at the joke, wishing he was someplace else, quite frankly anywhere else on this Saturday night. But his family had put their faith in him, and that faith had put their fortune at risk. Brody had made a bad calculation, and now it was up to him to set things right.

He was standing, while Quentin and Rex lounged in padded rattan chairs on the second level of the multitiered pool deck. Light spilled from the great room, its sliding glass walls wide open in the still August night as guests moved inside and out. Quentin liked to party, and the massive profits from his gaming company, Beast Blue Designs, ensured he had the means.

"Did you catch her baby owl tattoo?" Brody asked Rex, putting on the cocky confidence of the rock concert promoter he was pretending to be.

Rex looked surprised, causing Brody to suspect he hadn't bounced a quarter off or anywhere near the former Miss Ventura County's rear end.

Brody had caught a glimpse of the tattoo last Wednesday morning. It seemed Vera liked string bikinis and sunrise swims, while Brody had been the only punctual arrival at breakfast that day. It was all quite innocent, but he wasn't about to mess with his street cred by explaining the circumstance.

Quentin raised his highball in a toast. "Rock on, Brody."

"I do my best," Brody drawled.

"Take a seat," Quentin invited.

While Rex frowned at him, Brody eased onto another of the rattan chairs. Music from the extensive sound system throbbed around them. A few guests splashed in the pool, while others clustered around the bar and the dessert buffet.

"Well, hello there, gorgeous," Rex drawled, sitting up straight, prompting Brody to follow the direction of his gaze.

A new woman had appeared on the pool deck, leggy and tanned in sparkly four-inch heels. Her dress was a skintight wrap of hot, shimmering pink. Her short blond hair flowed sleekly around her face, purple highlights framing her thick-lashed, wide blue eyes. She wore sparkling earrings and chunky bangles. And when her bright red lips curved into a sultry smile, Brody felt the impact right down to his bones.

"Who is she?" he asked, before remembering to play it cool.

"Kate Dunhern," Quentin answered.

"Francie's sister?" Rex asked with clear surprise.

"It seems that's the little sister," said Quentin, a thoughtful thread running through his tone as he perused the woman with obvious curiosity.

"Who's Francie?" Brody asked, cataloging the women he'd met since striking up his acquaintance with Quentin. He didn't recall anyone named Francie.

"My baby-mama," said Quentin.

The revelation surprised Brody. "You have a child?"

"Annabelle."

Quentin had a daughter. Brody couldn't imagine how his research had overlooked that fact.

"How old is she?" he asked, looking to fill in the blanks while trying to imagine Quentin as a father.

Quentin glanced to Rex, as if he didn't know his own daughter's age.

"Around six months," Rex answered.

"I had no idea," Brody said.

"Why would you?" Rex asked, his smirk of superiority clearly intended to remind Brody he was a newcomer to this social circle, while Rex had known Quentin since junior high.

"She died last week," Quentin said in a matter-of-fact tone.

A sick feeling invaded Brody's stomach. "Your baby died?"

"Francie died," said Rex.

Brody was relieved, but then he was immediately sorry for Francie, and he was appalled by Quentin's apparently callous attitude toward the mother of his child. Not that he should have been surprised. Aside from the extravagant spending, what he knew so far was that Quentin Roo was cold, calculating and self-centered in just about every aspect of his life.

Brody's attention moved back to the jaw-dropping woman named Kate. He pondered her notice-me appearance. Her sister had died last week? And she was at a party, in a place like this, dressed like that? *Nice.*

"I'm sorry for your loss," Brody offered to Quentin.

Quentin gave a shrug. "She was fun, I suppose. But if she hadn't got knocked up, it would have been over a long time ago."

Just when Brody thought his opinion of Quentin couldn't sink any further, it did.

"Did she live here?" It seemed a long shot that Francie was involved in the Beast Blue Designs' intellectual property theft. But information was information, and Brody was gathering all he could.

"I let her use the gatehouse. Made it easier. I could sometimes see the kid when I had time."

Between drunken bashes? Brody bit back the sarcastic retort. Quentin's personal life was none of his business.

"What's the sister's story?" asked Rex, ogling Kate from the tips of her purple highlighted hair to the heels of her glittering sandals.

Brody found himself doing the same. He wasn't proud of the behavior, but he was mesmerized. Even in that gaudy getup, she was a knockout.

"Don't know," said Quentin. "Don't really care."

"She showed up out of the blue?" asked Rex.

"Apparently she came down from Seattle."

"Had you met her before?" Although this Kate person had nothing to do with his investigation into Quentin's gaming technology company, Brody found himself curious.

"Never even knew she existed," said Quentin.

Suspicion grew thick in Rex's tone. "So today was the first time you met her?"

"You want me to check her ID?"

"Being Francie's sister doesn't entitle her to anything," Rex said. "You can't hand out your money to every person who crosses your path."

"It's a whole lot easier than fighting them."

"It's stupid."

"Path of least resistance. Besides, the money train's not about to derail."

Brody clenched his jaw then downed the remainder of his Shet Select single malt. The taste grounded him, reminding him of his home in the Scottish Highlands, of his parents, his brother and his purpose for being here. Quentin's money train might still be going, but only because he'd ripped off the Calder family's technology.

Brody was here to prove Quentin had stolen from his family. And he was determined to send that money train right off the nearest cliff.

"You have better things to spend it on than opportunistic gold diggers," said Rex.

"Really? Name one." Quentin then turned his attention back to Vera, Miss Ventura County. "Think I'll get me a look at that baby owl."

Brody reminded himself to stay in character. He gave a salacious grin of approval to Quentin. "Go get 'er."

Quentin smiled in anticipation, polished off his martini and rose to his feet.

Two steps later, Kate Dunhern moved into his path.

"Hello, Quentin," she said.

Her tone was smooth, cultured, far different than Brody had expected. He thought he detected an underlying trace of nervousness. He wondered why she was nervous. Was she going to make a pitch for a payout right here and now?

"Hello, Kate," Quentin responded in a level tone. "Good to see you."

"Thanks for inviting me."

He gestured expansively around the deck. "It's a party."

"I wondered if there was somewhere we could talk?"

Quentin's gaze flicked back to the sexy Vera. "Depends on..."

While Kate obviously waited for him to finish the sentence, Vera caught his attention and sent a friendly smile his way.

"Maybe tomorrow," he said to Kate.

Though she tried to hide it, her disappointment was obvious. "Uh, sure. Okay."

"Catch you later." He moved past her.

Rex made to rise, but Brody was quicker. He didn't know what he hoped to gain from talking to the sister of a woman who'd had nothing to do with Beast Blue Designs, but he didn't want Rex hitting on her. He didn't know why he felt that way. But it didn't really matter.

He stepped up in front of her.

"Brody Herrington," he said, using the last name he'd temporarily adopted from his grandmother.

She took a long moment to focus on him. Then she

seemed to study him. While she did that, he detected an unexpected intelligence behind her eyes.

"Kate Dunhern," she finally responded.

"Can I get you a drink?"

She appeared to be gathering her bearings, even sizing him up. Then her mouth suddenly curved into a bright smile. In a flash, her assessing intellect was replaced by overexuberance and friendliness.

"Love one," she said. "Champagne?"

He couldn't help but puzzle at the cause of her transformation. Had she recognized his designer jeans? Had she noted his expensive watch and shoes and decided he was worth chatting up? Whatever it was, now she was behaving the way he'd expected when he first saw her purple-streaked hair and her crystal-studded sandals.

He offered his arm. "This way."

She took it, her bright pink manicured nails shimmering against his skin.

He did a double take at the distinctly sensual image and felt a spike of lust shoot through him. It was a normal reaction, he told himself. She was a gorgeous woman in an outfit designed to display it. She was likely disappointed at losing Quentin's attention, but she had the attention of every other red-blooded man here. If it was money she was after, there was plenty of it unattached and at the party.

"You're a friend of Quentin's?" she asked in a bright, friendly tone.

"An acquaintance," said Brody. He shouldn't, nor did he have any desire to lay claim to more.

"Are you in the video gaming business?"

"The entertainment industry. I'm a concert promoter from Europe."

"Scotland?" she guessed.

He'd wished he could keep it more generic, but his accent gave him away. He could only hope the fake profession and fake name would keep Quentin from making a connection to his father or, more significantly, to his family's ownership of Quentin's competitor Shetland Tech Corporation.

"You got me," he answered.

"I'm guessing it's not classical music you're promoting." Her gaze seemed to take in the party which was growing more raucous by the hour.

Brody knew it was only a matter of time until a fight broke out or someone got tossed into the pool. Breakage was a given. Quentin seemed to have a cleanup crew on perpetual standby to deal with whatever carnage was wrought at the late-night parties.

"Rock 'n roll," he answered.

"Anyone I might recognize?"

"Confidential, I'm afraid."

It was his pat answer whenever anyone pressed

for details. Luckily, so far nobody had probed further. He had enough money to buy credibility, and he doubted anybody really cared beyond that. He suspected most of the people in Quentin's circle lied about their background or profession in some way or another.

"Are you in LA for a concert?" she asked.

"I'm on vacation."

"Amusement parks and surfing?"

"Something like that. What about you?"

A cloud crossed her eyes. "You may have heard my sister was killed."

"I did." He wondered if he might have misjudged her. In this moment, her remorse struck him as genuine. "I'm sorry."

But then she seemed to shake off the melancholy. "We were estranged. I hadn't seen her in seven years."

They made it to the bar, and he placed their order—champagne for her and another Shet Select for him.

"Bad blood?" he asked, finding himself curious.

"Different goals and objectives in life." She accepted the flute of champagne.

"How so?"

She seemed to hesitate. "Hard to put my finger on it now." Then she grinned, the happy-go-lucky expression coming back into her eyes. "Interesting that she was with Quentin." The new tone was searching.

"Interesting," Brody agreed, thinking Quentin was probably right. Kate was here to trade on her sister's relationship with an enormously wealthy man.

"Quentin said you were down from Seattle," he continued.

"I live there."

"That wouldn't have been my first guess."

Her eyebrow arched. "Why not?"

"It doesn't seem like a very exciting town." His rock 'n roll alter ego jumped in. "And you seem like an exciting girl."

"Seattle might surprise you." She flashed a secretive smile, clinked her glass to his and turned to walk from the bar.

He could have let the conversation end there. It would have been the smart move. Kate was a distraction, and he didn't need any distractions right now. He was here to schmooze Quentin and the Beast Blue Designs team, get inside information on who was who and then pump them for details so he could prove they'd stolen intellectual property from Shetland Tech.

So far, his conversations with Scotland Yard and the LAPD had gotten him nowhere. Both police forces were focused on murders, kidnappings and drug crimes and had little time for possible corporate espionage. Not that he blamed them. They had to prioritize.

His second plan had been to hire a private investigator. But the guy they'd put undercover at Beast Blue Designs had been caught snooping, and the company was a veritable fortress of security and secrecy. He hadn't found out a single thing.

Running out of time, Brody had taken matters into his own hands. He was trying to gain Quentin's trust on a personal level to find a route into the company.

He told his feet to walk away from Kate. But they didn't.

"What do you do in Seattle?" he asked instead.

"This and that," she answered vaguely.

The answer likely meant she was unemployed, or perhaps embarrassed by her profession. Maybe she was a criminal, or a con artist, or simply a shameless opportunist.

Whatever she was, she was sexy as hell. He should be sprinting away from her and focusing on business. Instead, he eased closer, gazing into her blue eyes, touching his glass to hers a second time.

"To this and that," he said.

Two

The party was confirming Kate's worst fears. It was a rambunctious crowd, fuelled by throbbing techno music and excessive drinking. She was no expert, but she thought she detected the scent of marijuana wafting up from the gardens. And she feared there could be other recreational drugs being passed around Quentin's mansion.

She couldn't imagine what her sister had been thinking to bring a baby into an environment like this. On second thought, she supposed she knew exactly what Francie had been thinking: nothing, at least nothing beyond enjoying the next ten minutes of her life. She'd inherited that trait from Chloe.

As recently as this morning, Kate had convinced herself Annabelle would be fine. Chloe had sworn that Annabelle was the luckiest little girl in the world. Chloe had read all about Quentin Roo and was more than impressed with his money and his success.

He was in mourning now, she had said, and not ready to introduce Annabelle to anyone from the family. Impatient to get away from her childhood memories and back home again, Kate had been willing to buy into Chloe's optimism.

She'd made it as far as the airport, her bags checked, and arrangements made with Nadia to pick her up in Seattle. But while she waited for her flight to board she'd done an internet search and found some news items featuring Quentin. One showed him outside a downtown nightclub a few weeks back. He was clearly intoxicated, a sexy woman on his arm, confronting a police officer over the right to drive his fancy sports car.

Disturbed by the images, Kate had searched further. His social media presence painted a picture of a party animal. She also found clips of his belligerent behavior and descriptions of wild times held at his mansion. He might be rich, but he definitely wasn't responsible.

Protective instincts had welled up inside her. She'd cancelled her flight and left the airport, determined to confront him, determined to demand access to Annabelle and the right to ensure the baby was safe.

But halfway to his mansion, she'd stopped herself, realizing the confrontational approach was almost guaranteed to fail.

She knew she needed a better plan, something more subtle in order to get close to Annabelle without spooking Quentin. The best way she could think of to do that was appear amicable and nonthreatening, to fit seamlessly into his world. She'd decided the best option was to get to Quentin and pretend she was just like Francie.

One crazy makeover later, she did look like Francie. And now she was inside the party. And she'd met Quentin. Even if it was only momentarily, it was still a start.

The man named Brody kept pace with her along the pool deck. Whoops of delight echoed around them. Groups of people talked and laughed, drinks in hands, eyes alight with enthusiasm and exhilaration. The staccato of the bassline pummeled through to her bones.

She kept an eye on Quentin, waiting for the right moment to approach him again. He was engrossed in conversation with a tall blonde woman. She was model-thin, taller than Quentin, with impossibly long limbs and a gorgeous face that would do justice to any magazine cover.

"I've never been up north myself," Brody stated conversationally.

His deep, rolling accent purred over her. Ordinarily, she would have enjoyed that. But chatting up anyone but Quentin wasn't in her plans tonight, even if the man was distractingly attractive.

And Brody was definitely that. He had a strong chin with just enough beard stubble to be rakish. His eyes were slate gray, his brow quizzical, and he had a sexy dark shock of hair swooping across his forehead. His mouth was firm, slightly stern, some might even say judgmental. Although exactly what someone living in the thick of the rock-and-roll lifestyle would have to be judgmental about was a mystery to her.

"No rock concerts to promote in Washington State?" she asked, telling herself to keep it light and stay in character. Everybody with anything to do with Quentin needed to believe she was just like Francie, a girl looking to enjoy life without worrying too much about the details.

"North America is a secondary market. Here we mostly stick to New York City. I have been to Boston and Chicago, and once to Florida, but that was a vacation."

"Miami's a fun town." She was guessing. She'd

only ever seen it on television, but it seemed like a good bet.

She kept watch on Quentin, poised to interrupt as soon as she had a chance. She'd decided to down-play her interest in Annabelle tonight. A party girl wouldn't be fixated on a baby's welfare. But she was growing impatient. Quentin was getting rap-idly drunk, so who was with the baby?

"The Keys," Brody said beside her.

"What keys?" she asked.

"The Florida Keys."

"Oh." Kate told herself to focus and try to use the conversation productively. She'd track Annabelle down as soon as she could. "How long have you known Quentin?"

"I've been in LA for a few weeks," Brody replied. "But I've known of him for quite a bit longer."

She leaned casually against a rail that overlooked the sweeping lights of the city, keeping Quentin in her peripheral vision while the breeze blew her newly short hair back from her face. "And what do you think of him?"

Brody turned to face her. "In what sense?"

"I've seen the news reports, and I wonder how much of it is true."

He took in her outfit, and she was reminded of her heavy makeup, tight dress and the funky hair. She wasn't exactly comfortable with the impression she must be making, but she had to see this through.

"He knows how to have a good time," said Brody.

Kate gave her head a little toss and tried to look like a woman who was very much interested in having a good time. She glanced pointedly around the party, the pretty people, the exotic clothes, the expensive food and liquor. "This is definitely a good time."

There was an unfathomable expression in his eyes that could have been sarcasm or resignation. "Isn't it just."

The odd reaction made her curious. "You must be used to parties in your line of work."

"I've been to parties of all kinds."

"Wild ones?" she asked, striving to look intrigued and excited at the possibility.

"Some." He gave her a warm smile.

"Sounds terrific." She half expected him to toss out an invitation, at least a generic one: *maybe I'll take you sometime, baby...*

She'd refuse of course, politely. She wasn't here looking for dates. She was here for Annabelle and nothing else. But he didn't ask, and she found herself wondering if the purple highlights weren't working for her.

Just then Quentin left his conversation partner, and she spotted her opening. She made a quick move toward him, but her heel caught on a concrete seam, and she stumbled, sloshing her champagne.

Brody grasped her elbow, stabilizing her.

"Sorry." She quickly apologized for her clumsiness, hoping she hadn't splashed anything on his clothes.

"You all right?" he asked, still holding on to her.

"I tripped."

"You were in a pretty big hurry."

"I was—" She hesitated over her words. "I'm hoping to catch Quentin."

Brody glanced past her. "Someone beat you to him."

She turned to see two new women laughing with him. She cursed under her breath.

"He was just with your sister." There was censure in Brody's tone, and she looked up to see his gaze had hardened.

"It's not that." It was clear from his frown that he didn't believe her. "I'm not here to make a play for Quentin."

"You nearly injured yourself trying to get over there to chat him up."

"Not for that."

"Listen, it's not really any of my business."

"You're right. It's not. But I'm going to tell you anyway. I'm not romantically interested in Quentin."

She couldn't imagine any circumstance where she'd be romantically interested in a man like Quentin Roo.

Brody's gaze took a leisurely tour of her outfit. "Good news, Kate. Romance is not at all what you're projecting."

Despite the fact that she'd done so on purpose, she was offended by his implication that she'd dressed provocatively. "I'm not after Quentin in any way, shape or form."

"Of course you're not."

She didn't care what this Brody person thought. At least she shouldn't care about his opinion. But for some stupid reason, she did care.

It was on the tip of her tongue to explain that this was all about her niece. She was playacting here, making sure Annabelle was going to be okay. But she stopped herself just in time. Instead, she looked up at him and gave her highlighted hair another defiant toss. "I'm here for a good time."

His eyes reminded her of flints. "Aren't we all."

Brody watched the fleet of tiny electronic spaceships blast their way through an asteroid field on the wall-mounted wide screen. The ships changed colors, using different weapons, all jockeying for position while trying to avoid being annihilated by other players.

"See that? Right there," said Will Finlay, the head programmer from Shetland Tech. "The organics on the planet surface."

"All I see are a bunch of things exploding."

"It's the way they're exploding," said Will. "Or rather, the way they've changed the way they're exploding."

"If you say so." Brody wasn't a software engineer, and he wouldn't pretend to come close to Will's technical understanding.

"This is the best evidence yet. I've checked with a few contacts at MIT, and they agree Shetland Tech has been ripped off."

"Can we prove it with this?" Brody asked.

Will had managed to get his hands on a prototype of the Beast Blue Designs' new game, "Blue Strata Combat."

"Not without the source code," Will said. "We can prove they're using advanced algorithms that trigger object evolution within an AI environment, but we can't prove they stole it from Shetland."

"But they did," said Brody.

"They did."

"If we move now?"

"I'm told that if we make a move based on the evidence we have right now we'll be tied up in litigation for a few decades. And after that we'll probably lose."

Brody sat back in the burgundy leather armchair that was positioned in the living area of his hotel suite at the Diamond Pier Towers. He'd been away from home for over a month now, and he was growing impatient.

Back in Scotland, his brother Blane had too much to worry about already. Suffering from the neuromuscular disease Newis Bar Syndrome, Blane tired more easily than most people. But as eldest son, the Viscount and the future Earl of Calder, the responsibilities for the family seat fell to him. Brody had to at least take the money trouble out of the equation.

"We need to get inside their facility," Will said. "Proving our case still hinges on accessing their resident servers and finding our proprietary code."

"We already tried that."

The attempt had been a dismal failure. The technical security was impenetrable, and the server room was on lockdown twenty-four hours a day. The private detective they'd hired to go undercover as a technician was caught trying to gain unauthorized access and was summarily fired.

"Do you think Quentin might confess something?" Will asked.

"To me?"

"To anybody."

Brody found his thoughts moving to Kate. If he looked like Kate he might be able to get Quentin to spill his darkest secrets. But he didn't look like Kate, and so far Quentin didn't want to talk business with outsiders.

"I need to find an opportunity to search his house," Brody said. "If we can't get into their corporate headquarters, Quentin's house is the next best bet."

"You get caught snooping around? Well, I have to say, those security guys he's hired seem very serious."

"I'll be careful."

"They have Russian accents."

"I know."

Brody had heard rumors about Quentin's financial backers, that they had shady backgrounds and even shadier connections to overseas criminal organizations.

"I don't see we have any choice," he said.

"There's always a choice," Will said.

"You mean I can make the decision to bankrupt my family?"

"It's better than being shot."

"Marginally," Brody said.

Quite frankly, he'd rather take a bullet than be responsible for losing the Calder estate. The earldom had been in his family for twenty-two generations. They'd had ups and downs over the years. The land had been mortgaged before, but the family had always made it back to better times.

Five years ago, their financial position had become particularly precarious, and Brody knew they needed to modernize. His brother Blane, the viscount and eldest son of the earl, wanted to develop tourism infrastructure on the estate, starting with a hotel. But Brody worried about the high investment and slow rate of return that were part of Blane's plan. He knew they needed something faster, so he'd convinced his father to buy Will's start-up company and go into high-end gaming technology.

At first, it had worked brilliantly. They'd paid down their debt and were looking forward to moving into the tourism sector. But then Brody got overconfident. He'd borrowed again, borrowed more, and plowed the money into expanding Shetland Tech, creating a new game that he and Will were sure would revolutionize the industry.

Their logic was solid. So was their research. It should have been a success. It would have been a success. But then Beast Blue Designs had stolen their code and stood a frightening chance of beating them to market.

If Beast Blue succeeded, it would be impossible to

recoup Shetland Tech's sunk costs, and the company would most certainly go bankrupt. The Calder estate and the castle on the banks of the River Tay would be lost to the family forever.

"I'm serious," Will said, setting down the controller. "You can't mess with those guys."

"They already messed with me."

Will uttered an exclamation of disgust. "You're going to get all macho about it?"

"I'm not getting macho. What I'm getting is smart. If we can't infiltrate the company, then we'll come at it from another angle, through Quentin. The man drinks and parties to excess. He's not as sharp as he should be, and I've succeeded in becoming his new pal."

"That's because you're pretending to be exciting and likable."

"I like to think I'm generally both," Brody said with a straight face.

Will flashed a grin. "Right. Sure. Let's call you that. But you can't expect to meet Quentin Roo's standards."

"I'm definitely not the life of some parties," Brody said. He had absolutely no desire to be the life of Quentin's parties.

His phone buzzed on the low table in front of him. Will stayed silent while he picked it up.

"Blane," he answered warmly. He didn't have any good news for his brother, but he was still glad to hear from him.

Blane coughed into the phone. "Hi, Brody."

Brody was immediately concerned. "What's wrong? Are you ill?"

"I'm fine."

"You're sure?"

Blane coughed again. "It's nothing. Mother has me steaming in the bathroom."

Brody relaxed a little, since he knew that at the first sign of a problem their mother would hover over Blane. He glanced at his watch. "It's late there."

"Have you signed up to be my nanny?"

"If you're sick—"

"A tickle in my chest is not sick. I'm humoring her. I don't need to humor you."

"Okay."

"Oliver Masterson came by today."

The information gave Brody pause. Oliver Masterson was the head architect on the family's hotel development project. Oliver shouldn't have much to do at the moment, because it was a long-term plan, with nothing substantive happening for years down the road. Brody thought they were all clear on the timing.

He spoke to his brother in a cautious tone. "We're only looking for preliminary drawings right now."

"We were. We are," said Blane. "He only wanted to see the site. He likes the view of the lake."

"Who wouldn't?"

The east meadow was one of Brody's favorite spots on the entire three-hundred-acre estate. If he'd had his way, they'd have built a house there and turned the castle into a hotel. But his mother wouldn't hear of moving from the family's traditional home.

"He wants the building to go higher," said Blane.

"Higher than three stories?"

"I know that puts us into a whole new category of construction. But we need to think of the long term, our children's children and beyond. The high-end market provides the best return on investment."

"You've been talking to the town council again." A large, five-star hotel on the Calder lands would have spin-off effects to any number of local businesses.

Blane coughed again. "You know they're right."

"I understand where you're coming from, Blane."

"And you agree with me."

Brody did agree. Like their ancestors before them, they had an obligation to support the surrounding community. He agreed there was growth potential in luxury tourism. The only problem he had was cash flow. They needed significant cash to flow in order to underwrite his brother's dream. Right now, they didn't have it.

"Don't sign anything today," he said.

"I won't. Are you close?" Blane knew only the broad strokes of the problem with Beast Blue Designs. He didn't know how precarious their financial situation had become.

"Getting closer," said Brody, knowing he was going to have to make something happen soon or confess to his family the full extent of their problems.

"Let me know how it goes." Blane's coughing started again.

"I will. Get better."

Blane wheezed out a laugh. "I'm in good hands."

Brody couldn't help but smile as he set down the phone. Their mother the countess was a force of nature.

"Problem?" asked Will.

"They want to make the hotel bigger."

"Let me guess. They accomplish that by spending more money."

"I knew you weren't just a pretty face." Brody suddenly felt tired and momentarily defeated. "It's always about more money. We need to win this thing, Will. And we need to do it soon."

"Okay," said Will, squaring his shoulders. "Let's hope Quentin is the kind of guy who brings his work home with him. If you can get in front of his home computer, I can tell you what to look for. But don't get caught, and whatever you do don't get shot by the Russian bodyguards."

Brody frowned. "I have no intention of getting shot."

"Nobody *plans* to get shot," said Will. "It happens all of a sudden and usually at the most inconvenient time."

Three

Kate had wrangled an invitation back to Quentin's Sunday night. She had been hoping to talk to him alone and maybe even meet Annabelle. But she'd been disappointed on both fronts.

Annabelle had been put to bed by the nanny before Kate arrived, and Quentin didn't even show his face. His friends didn't seem to care, though, guzzling liquor, dancing on the furniture and frolicking in the pool to music from a live band in the gazebo.

She'd had no desire to party, but she was more determined than ever to meet Annabelle. So when she saw a woman passed out on a sofa, she'd come up with an idea. As the party wore down, she found a quiet corner and pretended to do the same.

There was no way she was dozing off amidst intoxicated strangers. So she lay there awake until 4:00 a.m. when the last guests had stumbled away.

Chilled and exhausted, she'd finally closed her eyes.

At five, the cleaners showed up and began straightening the furniture and clearing up the debris—empty bottles, broken glass, garbage and cigarette butts discarded everywhere. At six, they turned on vacuum cleaners and began to filter the pool water.

Giving up on the idea of sleeping, Kate found a bathroom. She gazed at her smudged makeup, mussed hair and the dark circles under her eyes. Lack of sleep made her look exactly like a woman who'd partied too hard two nights in a row. It was depressing, but there was no denying it would help her disguise. She ran a comb through her hair and wiped away the worst of the mascara smudges, then her thoughts turned to coffee.

As she moved down the hallway, she heard a woman's voice chirping happily about it being a beautiful day and how she was warming a bottle that would be delicious. Kate guessed it had to be the nanny talking to Annabelle. Her chest swelled with anticipation, and she picked up her pace, following the voice.

"You look so pretty this morning," the nanny singsonged. "Such a smiley girl."

Kate moved through the archway into a bright, airy

kitchen, to see a young woman in blue jeans and an orange T-shirt, holding a baby against one shoulder and a bottle in the opposite hand.

"Are you hungry?" the young woman asked Annabelle in a gentle voice, and then she spotted Kate.

"Oh," she said, her expression sobering. "Hello. I didn't realize anyone was here."

"Leftover from last night," Kate offered in an apologetic tone, smoothing a hand over her messy hair.

"Can I help you with something?" the woman asked, her voice and manner becoming reserved.

Kate couldn't keep her gaze from Annabelle. The baby girl had blond hair and big blue eyes in a sweet, delicate-looking face. Her pink mouth was perfect, and she was dressed in a white romper dotted with colored hearts.

"I'm..." Kate struggled for words. "I was hoping to meet Annabelle."

The woman's gaze narrowed, and she drew almost imperceptibly back.

Kate was reminded of how she looked and of the impression she must be giving.

"I'm Kate Dunhern," she quickly put in. "Francie's sister."

When the woman didn't immediately respond, it occurred to Kate that she might be new on the job.

"Did you know Francie?" Kate asked.

"I didn't know she had a sister." The woman was still obviously cautious.

"We weren't close."

"She never mentioned you."

Kate kept her voice calm and mild. She didn't mind that the nanny was protective. "I can answer some questions about Francie. Or I can show you some identification."

The offers seemed to dispel the woman's fears. "That won't be necessary. I'm Christina Alder, Annabelle's nanny."

"I guessed that," said Kate, taking a step forward. "She's adorable."

Christina smiled fondly at Annabelle. "Isn't she? She's a sweetheart, good as gold."

"Have you been taking care of her long?" Kate moved closer still, taking it slow, smiling at Annabelle, trying not to startle the baby.

"From the day she was born," said Christina.

Kate reached out and touched Annabelle's little hand with her finger.

"Baa," said Annabelle.

"Baa, yourself." Kate smiled. "I'm your auntie Kate."

Annabelle wiggled, and Christina shifted her hold. "You're a friend of Quentin's?" asked Christina.

Kate shook her head. "I only just met him on Saturday. I came home for…" She paused. "Well, I was disappointed they didn't have a service for Francie. And then I learned about Annabelle."

Annabelle wrapped her fist around Kate's index finger, and a shaft of warmth shot straight to Kate's heart.

"She misses her mommy," said Christina. But there was something off in her tone, as if she was being polite rather than sincere.

"It's good that she has you."

"Yes," said Christina, sounding more sincere. "It helps."

"And there's Quentin," said Kate, opening the door for a comment about Quentin's abilities as a father.

"There are a lot of demands on his schedule." Christina's tone was neutral.

"He seems very busy."

"He is very busy." Christina paused. "He loves his daughter, though."

"I'm sure he does."

Annabelle started to squirm, and her face twisted into a frown.

"She's hungry," said Christina.

"I'm sorry I interrupted."

"Not at all. I just need to sit down to feed her."

Kate stepped back to give them some room. She

wasn't sure if she should leave, but she desperately wanted to stay.

Christina climbed into a padded chair at the breakfast bar and adjusted Annabelle across one forearm, popping the bottle into the baby's mouth. Annabelle began to suck and her eyes fluttered closed.

"She's very patient," said Christina. "Most babies cry from the time you get them up to the time they get their bottles."

"Have you cared for a lot of babies?"

"I've had my diploma for four years. I did a lot of fill-in work for the first two, and my last posting was newborn twins." Christina smiled. "They were a handful." She smoothed a lock of hair across Annabelle's forehead.

"Boys or girls?" asked Kate, easing her way onto one of the other chairs.

"Boys. We got them into a routine at about four months. Mom took them on by herself when they hit six months. She still sends me email updates."

"They're doing well?" Kate continued to watch Annabelle.

"They just had their first birthday. They're finally both sleeping through the night." Christina sobered. "I'm very sorry about your sister."

"Me, too," said Kate. "I hadn't seen her in a long time. Well, I guess you would know that since I haven't been to see Annabelle. I didn't even know Francie was pregnant."

Christina didn't respond to that. Kate supposed there wasn't a whole lot more to say on the subject.

"I'm glad she had Annabelle and Quentin in her life," said Kate.

Christina's brow furrowed ever so slightly "You know we lived in the gatehouse, right?"

Kate wasn't sure what that meant. "The gatehouse?"

"Quentin and Francie, they weren't... They weren't together as a couple. He said he liked having Annabelle close by, but I understood his relationship with Francie was short-lived." Christina glanced away, as if she was aware that she'd shared too much.

"Thanks for telling me that. I didn't know."

Cristina didn't answer, instead adjusting the bottle at Annabelle's mouth.

"It was nice that Francie could live here," said Kate, glancing around at the huge, ultramodern kitchen.

From where she sat, she could see the estate grounds and the city beyond. The great room was behind her with its expensive furniture and art, the plush carpeting and a massive stone fireplace across one entire wall. If the gatehouse was any comparison to the main house, Francie had lived in the lap of luxury.

"She did enjoy the lifestyle," said Christina.

Kate could well imagine, at least from what she remembered of her sister. "Quentin seems to throw her kind of parties."

"He does," said Christina, removing the bottle from Annabelle's mouth and holding the baby against her chest to pat Annabelle's back. "She definitely liked the nightlife better than the mornings."

"I remember that about her."

"But she had me. So she didn't need to worry about the mornings."

A male voice interrupted their conversation. "Sorry to barge in."

Kate stood, turning to see the man she'd met Saturday night.

Brody Herrington looked a whole lot fresher than she felt in her crumpled cocktail dress. He'd topped a pair of well-worn jeans with a crisp charcoal dress shirt.

"I wouldn't have taken you for an early riser," he said to Kate.

She stuck to her story. "The vacuuming woke me up."

"I'll get out of your way," said Christina, her demeanor immediately changing to deference as she rose with Annabelle.

Kate wanted to tell her not to leave, to ask her to

please stay and talk some more. She wanted to learn about her sister and Annabelle's life here with Quentin. But she couldn't risk tipping her hand. If Quentin knew she was here to judge his fitness as a parent, he would send her packing.

"It was nice to meet you," she said instead.

Christina gave her a brief nod and left the room.

"You crashed here last night?" Brody asked.

"One too many martinis," Kate lied, pushing past her embarrassment to stay in character.

What must he think of a woman who passed out at a party? Then she told herself he probably didn't think anything. He likely met that kind of woman all the time.

"I may have left my watch behind last night," he said, holding up his bare wrist as evidence. Then he seemed to spy a coffeepot. He smiled and crossed to it.

"Want some?" he asked.

"Kill for some."

He retrieved a pair of mugs from a glassed-in cupboard. "I was going to take a look around and see if I could find it."

"It must be expensive," she observed.

He looked puzzled. "Expensive?"

"You're here at six in the morning. I assume you were worried about it."

"Oh. Yes. Well, it is a nice watch. It was a gift. From my mother on my twenty-first birthday. It's engraved."

"So, sentimental value."

"Sentimental value," he agreed as he poured the coffee.

The revelation surprised Kate. Brody didn't seem like the sentimental type.

"You need anything in it?" he asked.

"Black is fine."

He held out one of the mugs, and she moved to take it. In addition to a movie-star-handsome face, he had the most extraordinary eyes. They were dark and deep, slate gray in some lights, shot with silver in others. Right now they seemed to shimmer with contemplation. For a second she worried he saw right through her disguise.

"Want some help?" she asked, more to break the silence than anything else.

"Help?"

"To find your watch."

"Oh. Sure. It has a black face and a platinum band."

She couldn't help but grin at that. "To help me distinguish it from all the other watches lying around the mansion?"

"It was a great party."

"Yes, it was," she lied.

She simply couldn't understand the appeal of such a rowdy event. It was impossible to carry on a conversation over the loud music, music that grated in her ears. The guests were all drunk or high and only interested in gossip and fashion and bragging about their money or their connections.

"You don't say that with a lot of conviction," Brody observed.

She covered her expression with a swallow of the coffee. It tasted fantastic. "I guess I'm still recovering from the fun."

"You do look a little rough around the edges."

"Aren't you suave."

"You want me to lie?"

"Sure. Why not?"

His dark eyes warmed with humor. "You look fantastic this morning."

"Lukewarm delivery. But I'll take it."

His gaze moved downward, noting her one-shouldered, jeweled, sea-foam cocktail dress. It was tight and stiff and terrible to sleep in.

"I like the dress," he said.

"It's too late for you to try to flirt with me."

"I disagree."

"Then it's too early for you to flirt with me." She took another satisfying swallow of the coffee. "Chat me up later, when my brain is fully functional."

"I'll hold you to that."

Kate knew flirting with Brody was a mistake. She needed to keep him and everyone else at arm's length.

"Where did you last see it?" she asked him.

"See what?"

"Your watch."

"Oh, right." He glanced around. "I don't know. I'm not sure. I was going to start with the great room."

She polished off her coffee. "Lead on."

Kate decided that looking for Brody's watch was a plausible reason to hang around the mansion a while longer. She might get another chance to see Annabelle or a chance to talk to Quentin. Thus far, she hadn't managed to get the man to stand still long enough to have more than a ten-second conversation.

Brody pulled up the sofa cushions, checking behind each one. Kate took the opposite end of the room, scanning the floor, the tabletops, the windowsills, eventually making her way into the dining room and hunting around its corners. The cleaners were still working and nodded politely to her as they passed. They seemed used to encountering leftover party guests.

It occurred to her they would assume she'd had a companion last night. After all, that was the most common reason for a woman to be dressed in a cock-tail dress in the early hours of the morning. She told herself not to care. But then she found herself wondering if Brody thought the same thing.

Had he believed her when she said she'd fallen asleep? Did he think she'd had a one-night stand? He might even think she spent the night with Quentin.

She shuddered at the very idea.

She told herself again not to care what Brody thought. What Brody thought of her was completely irrelevant. Still she found herself retreating to the great room to set the record straight.

He wasn't there.

She listened, but she didn't hear anything. So she headed down the hall, toward the main staircase, glancing into the rooms with open doors. She found Brody in an office, standing behind a desk plunking the keys of a computer.

"Find anything?" she asked.

He looked guiltily up, and she couldn't help but wonder what he was doing.

"Nothing," he answered.

She waited to see if he'd elaborate.

"I was taking a quick check of my emails." He hit a couple more keys. "We've got a big tour in the works."

"Sounds exciting."

He shrugged. "Fairly routine. But you know rock stars."

"Big egos?" she guessed.

"Big everything. They need a lot of TLC." He moved from behind the desk.

She struggled for an opening to broach the subject, but there was no way to nonchalantly work it in. She decided to tackle it head-on. "I did fall asleep last night."

"Huh?"

"What I said earlier. That was how it happened. I had a few too many drinks and accidentally fell asleep on a sofa."

His gaze narrowed, and he looked intrigued.

"I was telling you the truth," she said.

"Okay."

"Was that sarcasm?" She couldn't tell if he believed her or not.

"That was. It's none of my business."

"I wasn't with Quentin."

Brody looked so genuinely surprised that she felt foolish.

She tried to backpedal. "I was remembering what you said Saturday night. You seemed to...well, allude to me possibly being after Quentin in an unsavory way."

"You said you weren't."

"I'm not."

"I believed you." He seemed sincere.

Now she really felt foolish. "Good. That's good." She told herself to stop talking, but for some reason she kept on. "Why?"

He flexed an amused grin, brushing his fingers along the top of the wooden desk as he moved toward her. "You didn't look like you were lying."

"How does lying look?" What was the matter with her? She sounded silly, and she didn't seem to be able to quit. "I mean to you. How can you tell?"

"I don't know. How does anyone tell?" He stopped in front of her.

It was too close for comfort, but she didn't move.

"Lack of eye contact," he continued. "A tense, closed expression, halting speech, hesitation."

He certainly didn't look tense. He looked relaxed. He looked powerful, in control, and too, too sexy. She should look away and break the spell. She didn't.

"Take now," he said, leaning ever so slightly forward. "Your expression is open. You're not nervous. You're looking straight at me. It's like you're inviting me in."

Uh-oh.

"Like you want me to see your innermost thoughts," he continued.

She definitely didn't want that. Her innermost thoughts were her business and hers alone.

"Like you're thinking physical contact..." He brushed her fingers, gently holding the tips of hers with the tips of his. He drew in a deep breath. "Wouldn't be a bad thing."

She felt a warmth rise over her wrist, up the inside of her arm and through to her chest. She didn't want him to let go.

He eased in, his intention clear. His hand wrapped itself fully around hers, intensifying the sensations. She lost track of time and place, forgot about everything but Brody as he drew her close.

His lips touched hers. The kiss was gentle. She hadn't expected that. His free hand came to rest at her waist, again the lightest of touches. If he'd kissed her hard or pulled her fast and tight, she might have had the presence of mind to break away. But he was stealthy in his approach, slipping past her defenses, his actions so soothing that she didn't realize her mistake.

The kiss deepened.

It felt good. It felt great.

She stepped forward, bringing her body against his, chest to chest, thigh to thigh. His hand moved along the small of her back, splaying warm and smooth against her spine.

Her lips parted, and he groaned, pulling back, breaking the kiss.

"I'm sorry," he said.

She felt her face heat in embarrassment. "No, I'm sorry. I shouldn't—"

Then she remembered the part she was supposed to be playing. Girls like Francie didn't get rattled by a kiss. So instead of apologizing, she gave him a sultry smile and walked her fingers down his chest before dropping her hand to her side. "No problem. Just so we're clear on Quentin."

Brody looked confused for a moment. Then he seemed to give himself a little shake. "Glad we got that out of the way."

She wanted to ask him if it was the question of Quentin that was now out of the way, or if their kiss was the thing that was out of the way. Had he been curious about kissing her? Had he been disappointed? Was he moving on?

A dozen questions bloomed in her mind, but she couldn't ask any of them. The kiss was definitely out of the way. It was done. She was moving past it, past Brody, and back on to Annabelle.

Four

Brody heard deep voices in the mansion hallway and kicked himself for getting distracted by Kate. She was gorgeous and sexy, and who could blame him for kissing her. But he'd let his guard down. Quentin's computer was still on, and somebody was approaching.

It sounded like two of them. Their voices were guttural, speaking in Russian, Quentin's security guards for sure.

He grasped Kate's arm and drew her out of sight. "What?" she started to ask.

"Shhh," he cautioned.

She looked puzzled but stopped talking. For that, he was grateful.

The voices rose. The footsteps paused by the door.

He pressed himself and Kate flat against the wall, ready to kiss her again if the men came into the room. He assumed a clandestine sexual encounter would be something they'd understand and accept.

Luckily, instead of looking in, they resumed walking and talking.

Kate whispered, "Are we doing something wrong?"

"No," he lied.

He was definitely doing something wrong. She thought she was searching for his lost watch.

"I didn't want to embarrass you," he lied again.

"Embarrass me how?"

He made a show of taking in her outfit from last night.

"Oh." She wrapped her arms around her front, covering her cleavage and bare shoulders. "They'd think I spent the night with you."

"They would."

"Thanks, then."

"No problem."

A split second later, she gave a little shrug, dropping her hands to her sides. "But what would I care?"

It was a good question. He wasn't sure why he thought she'd care about the opinions of strangers. He did know pretending to be chivalrous was a whole lot better than explaining to her that he'd been checking out Quentin's computer.

"Who are they?" she asked, still keeping her voice low.

"Security guards. Quentin has a lot of them. Every one brawny, ill-humored and uncommunicative."

"What did they mean that Quentin had better be persuaded?"

The question surprised Brody. No, not surprised. It shocked the heck out of him. "You speak Russian?"

"No. But they were speaking Ukrainian."

That was another surprise. All along, he'd thought the guys were Russian.

He gave her a beat to elaborate.

She didn't.

"Same question," he prompted.

"Only a little. I understand it better than I speak it." She moved away from the wall, peeping out the open door.

"And?" he asked, struggling to keep the impatience from his tone. "That's because?"

"Oh. My best friend Nadia is Ukrainian. She grew up with her grandmother who lived across the hall from our apartment. Mrs. Ivanova was a crotchety old thing, and she didn't speak much English. She wore baggy stockings and embroidered cloth shoes, but I liked her because she baked incredible honey cookies and Kiev cake."

"And she taught you Ukrainian?"

Kate seemed to have a peculiar way of getting around to a point.

"Nadia and I tried to teach her English," said Kate. "Turns out, we weren't very good teachers."

"But you were a good student?"

She made a tipping motion with her hand. "I was okay. Nadia's fluent. I dabble."

"You understood those two."

"Only part of it."

"What else?" Brody didn't want to drag an unsuspecting Kate into his web of intrigue. But what she'd overheard could be important.

There were rumors Quentin had originally been financed by an Eastern European criminal organization. Assuming the rumors were true, Brody had wondered if the bodyguards might be connected to the financier. If they were, maybe they were into other kinds of crime, like corporate espionage.

One thing was sure: given the snippet of conversation Kate had interpreted, there was a real chance those men were more than just bodyguards.

"I didn't understand most of it," she said. "And I might be getting it wrong."

He tried not to sound too earnest. "What exactly did you hear?"

"That Quentin could be or maybe had to be persuaded. Something about him accepting or maybe embracing Ceci."

"Ceci?"

"That's what I heard."

Who was Ceci? "Did they mention a last name?"

"No."

"Accepting her as what?"

"A girlfriend, maybe?"

"They said that?"

"I'm tossing out random guesses," she said.

"What about the context?"

"I'm not that good."

"But—"

"Brody, it was a tiny snippet of conversation in a foreign language from a distance. What do you want from me?"

He immediately regretted grilling her. "You're right. I'm sorry."

"Why do you care so much?"

"I don't." He ordered himself to take a beat and relax. "You had me curious is all. I've listened to those guys talk amongst themselves for weeks now and never knew what they were saying."

She peered at him for a moment, seeming to assess

his expression. Once again, she appeared smarter than he would have guessed. But then she blinked, and the expression was gone.

"Maybe that's why he broke up with Francie," she speculated aloud. "To be with this Ceci person."

"I've never seen him with a steady girlfriend." Then again, Brody hadn't ever come across Francie, either. There could be any number of people in Quentin's life that Brody didn't know about.

"Do you suppose he has another child?" asked Kate. "Maybe those guys want him to marry Ceci because they have a baby."

That seemed like a long shot to Brody, and not at all helpful to his investigation. He wanted the bodyguards and the mysterious Ceci to be clues to Beast Blue Designs' theft from Shetland. Though he acknowledged that was a long shot, as well.

The thought did remind him of why he was here and what he was doing. He needed to get back at it.

"No sign of my watch in here," he said to Kate. "Did you happen to check the dining room?"

She nodded. "I did."

"What about the kitchen?" He wanted to get her out of the office so that he could turn off Quentin's computer.

"Would you like me to check there?"

"That would help. I was in there a few times last night."

"I'm surprised I didn't see you at the party."

"I spent most of the evening in the garden." Lying was becoming easier and easier for him. He wasn't sure how he should feel about that.

He hadn't even been at last night's party, never mind lost his watch. It was a ruse he'd concocted as an excuse to snoop around the mansion. It wasn't the most complicated plan in the world, but he'd decided simpler was better.

She seemed to expect him to elaborate on his statement.

"With a woman," he lied again. "Somebody I just met."

A bit of the friendliness vanished from her expression. "Right."

He wanted to tell her he was lying. He wasn't like Quentin and the rest of the partiers. He didn't have sex in the garden with random women. But telling her the truth was dangerous. Like everybody else in this world, she needed to believe he was Brody Herrington, a freewheeling concert promoter living the rock-and-roll lifestyle.

If one surprisingly interesting woman thought he was some kind of a player, then that was the price he'd pay.

"I'll check the kitchen," she said, turning away.

"Kate?"

She stopped without turning back. "Yes?"

He knew he was selfish to ask for her cooperation, but his family was at stake. "Don't let on."

She twisted her head to look at him.

"Don't let on that you understand Ukrainian."

Her brow furrowed in puzzlement.

"I don't trust those guys." That much was definitely true. "It's probably better if you just listen." He wished he could ask her to report back to him on what she heard, but he didn't dare go that far.

"I wasn't planning to let on," she said.

"Good."

"I'll go check for your watch."

"Thanks."

"Maybe if you kept your clothes on," she muttered under her breath. "You might not lose things."

He watched her walk away, her hair slightly mussed, her shoulders bare, her legs long and shapely beneath the tight, short dress. It struck him as odd that she'd criticize his behavior. But a split second later, she only struck him as gorgeous, and he forgot about anything else.

Kate took a quick look through the kitchen, and then decided Brody could find his own watch. It was probably in the garden, falling off when he'd stripped down for a quickie.

It had annoyed her to learn he'd spent the evening hooking up. She acknowledged the reaction was absurd, since it had absolutely nothing to do with her. With his job, he probably had one-night stands all over the world—him and all the other single, wealthy men hanging out with celebrities and groupies.

But for some reason she wanted him to be better than the rest. Maybe it was because she'd kissed him. Or more important because she'd enjoyed kissing him. She should have better taste than to enjoy kissing a man who was into one-night stands. What was the matter with her?

She made her way back into the main hallway, focusing on Annabelle again, and wondering how long she dared hang around. She didn't want anyone to get suspicious, but she also didn't want to squander this opportunity.

Time was ticking. Banking on Quentin being a late sleeper, she decided to have a look upstairs before she left.

She guessed Annabelle's nursery would be on the second floor and hoped Christina and Annabelle had gone back there when they left the kitchen. If anyone questioned her, she could always use the excuse of Brody's lost watch.

At the top of the stairs, she heard the gentle pings of a lullaby. She walked toward them, coming to an open bedroom door.

Annabelle was lying in a white crib, cooing softly, her hands and bare feet wiggling in the air as she watched colorful cloth jungle animals circle above her.

The rest of the big room was a jumble, containing a change table, two armchairs, a rocking chair. Through an open doorway to a connected room, she saw a single bed and a dresser. Everything was covered in cardboard boxes. Some were open, some taped shut. Plush toys were strewn around the nursery, and the walk-in closet was wide-open, revealing empty shelves and more packing boxes.

"Wow," said Kate. "You've got some work on your hands."

Christina looked surprised by the sound of Kate's voice.

Kate knew she was being unforgivably brazen barging in on them. She squelched her discomfort. "Do you want some help?"

"That's not necessary."

"I'm happy to do it." Kate forced herself to ignore Christina's obvious lack of welcome, moving to one of the open boxes of baby clothes to look inside. "Shall I put these in the closet?"

"No, really." Christina started toward her.

Annabelle let out a cry.

"I'll get her," Kate impulsively announced.

"No," Christina said sharply.

Their gazes met.

Kate realized she couldn't pull it off. Maybe in the midst of a party she could pretend to be self-centered and oblivious to the needs of others. But she couldn't do that to Christina.

"I'm sorry," she said. She took a step back. "I don't mean to put you in an awkward position." She took another step back, steadying herself on the doorjamb. "I wanted to see Annabelle is all. I'll leave the two of you in peace."

Disappointment running through her, Kate turned for the door.

"Wait," said Christina.

Kate paused and turned back.

Christina took a deep breath. "I'm not trying to be suspicious. It's just that most of Quentin's friends are…"

"Untrustworthy?" Kate guessed.

"I try to keep Annabelle out of their paths. They think she's a toy, and they're not always…"

"Sober?"

Christina looked stricken. "I shouldn't be saying these things."

"I'm not like them." Kate realized she was ready to come clean with Christina.

"Not like who?" Quentin appeared in Kate's peripheral vision.

For a second, her heart lodged in her throat. How much had he overheard? She scrambled for a plausible response.

"Not like those uptight people who hate mess and noise." She gave a brilliant smile.

Christina looked confused.

"You mean the Vernons?" asked Quentin.

"Who are the Vernons?"

"The people next door. Did they complain about the music again?"

"I loved the music," said Kate. "But, I fell asleep on the sofa. Too many martinis. My bad." She gave a giggle.

"There's no such thing as too many martinis," said Quentin.

Annabelle let out another cry, and Quentin winced at the sound.

"Now that kind of noise will make a man nuts."

Christina moved quickly to shush the baby.

Kate bit back a reproach. He shouldn't blame a baby for crying.

"Do you have parties every weekend?" she asked instead.

He gave a shrug. "People tend to drop by."

She wanted to ask how that was going to work with Annabelle living in the main house, but she held back.

One of the bodyguards appeared beside Quentin, holding out a cell phone. "Mr. Kozak for you."

Quentin clenched his jaw. Mr. Kozak was obviously not someone Quentin was pleased to hear from.

The bodyguard met Quentin's annoyed expression with a level stare.

"Not now," said Quentin.

The bodyguard stayed silent. He waited, obviously expecting Quentin to change his mind.

Kate could feel the tension in the air.

"Tell him I'll call him back," said Quentin.

After a long moment, the bodyguard turned abruptly, raising the phone to his ear. He spoke in Ukrainian as he walked away, but it was too fast. Kate couldn't make out any of the words.

Christina had moved to the far side of the room, jiggling Annabelle in her arms and cooing softly in her ear.

Annoyance was radiating from Quentin.

Kate's stomach clenched, and her instincts told her to leave, to get out of the room, even out of the house. She didn't know what was going on here, but Quentin clearly had a temper. She had no desire to be in

his line of fire. But she didn't want to leave Annabelle and Christina alone with him.

"I, uh…" She scrambled to think what Francie
would do.

After only a second, she came up with a plausible
solution. Francie would have been completely oblivious to the undercurrents. She'd be thinking solely of
herself. What was Francie feeling? What did Francie want?

Kate was exhausted, and she was hungry. She went
with it.

"Any way to get some breakfast around here?" she
asked him coyly.

Quentin looked taken aback. But his surprised expression didn't last long. He seemed willing to be
distracted.

"You're hungry?" he asked.

"Famished. I usually have blueberry muffins for
breakfast," she rattled off. "Except on Sundays. On
Sundays I go to this little bistro on Backwater Street.
It's about a block from the ocean, and they have the
best eggs Benedict I have ever eaten." She grinned
invitingly. "With a mimosa. To die for, really."

Quentin's expression had relaxed.

She couldn't help thinking it was easy being Francie. There was no need to worry about empathy or

propriety or even good manners. You just led with your emotions and lived in the moment.

"Eggs Benedict it is," he said. He gestured to the nursery doorway.

Kate was disappointed to leave Annabelle. But in the short term, getting into Quentin's good graces was the most important thing. If she played her cards right, she'd have time to see Annabelle again later.

"You have a really gorgeous house," she told him as they walked down the hallway. She ran her fingertips along the white panel molding.

"I bought it from Deke Hamilton," he said.

"The movie star?" She put what she hoped was the right amount of awe and admiration into the question.

"He had it custom built," said Quentin. "Cost ten million, but I got it for nine."

"Nice."

"The divorce."

Kate wished she could remember something about Deke Hamilton's love life, but she couldn't.

"You always lose money on a divorce," she said.

"True that," said Quentin. "I'll sure never fall for it."

"Marriage?" she guessed.

"Marriage, common-law, palimony. Whatever."

It occurred to her that was probably why Francie

and Annabelle had lived in the gatehouse. Quentin didn't want to risk a lawsuit. She couldn't help but think he had to have plenty of money to spare.

As they descended the stairs, she pointed to a huge, dramatic crystal chandelier. "Swarovski?" she asked, dredging up the only famous name she knew.

"Of course."

She tilted her head to admire it.

"Are you here for Francie's things?" he asked.

The question surprised Kate. She hadn't thought of that. But she realized it was a fair assumption. The woman Kate was pretending to be would probably covet anything Quentin might have bought for Francie.

Then again, if by "things" he meant Annabelle, the answer was rapidly turning into a yes.

She put a speculative gleam in her eyes, and a faux coy tone in her voice. "What things?"

Quentin laughed, clearly pleased with himself for having guessed her motive.

Kate was happy to let him think he had her figured out.

"You seem like a generous man," she said, playing it up even further.

"I just told you I'd never get married and risk alimony," he responded.

"True," she conceded. "But that doesn't mean you don't like to make women happy."

Brody's voice joined the conversation. "I assure you, he does."

Brody's gaze was judgmental as he peered at Kate, and her heart fluttered in a nervous reaction. He was going to think the worst of her all over again.

She didn't care, she told herself one more time. She couldn't and wouldn't care.

"Brody's got me pegged," said Quentin. "What about you?" he asked Brody. "You willing to risk it all for some woman?"

"Depends on the woman."

Quentin laughed. "I can't even picture who that would be."

Kate found herself waiting for Brody's answer.

"Tall," he said. "Large breasts and big hair."

She involuntarily glanced down at her chest. No, not so much. Plus, she was only five feet five, and her hair was sleek rather than puffy, shorter than it had been three days ago. And he hadn't mentioned liking a woman's hair to be purple, so she supposed she was nowhere near his demographic.

"You'll want to visit Texas," said Quentin, chuckling.

"I'll think about it," said Brody.

She supposed she could wear high shoes and a

wig, but she drew the line at cosmetic surgery. Her breasts were staying the size they were.

Not that she wanted to attract Brody. He kissed very well, but she didn't want it to happen again. Okay, so she did want it to happen again. But that was an emotional reaction, nothing based on reason. It was definitely better all around if it didn't happen again, not ever. Logic told her that. And she was nothing if not logical.

"I'm saving the jewelry," Quentin said to Kate.

"Huh?" She wasn't following him.

"I'm saving Francie's jewelry for Annabelle."

Kate told herself to look disappointed. "Oh."

"That seems fair," said Brody.

Kate agreed, but she didn't chime in with her agreement. It was better if Quentin thought she was opportunistic and greedy instead of judging his fitness as a father. She switched to a safer topic, again trying to be Francie-like.

"We're having eggs Benedict," she said to Brody. "Because I'm famished."

He looked bemused by the observation.

Rex, who Kate had learned that first night was Quentin's right-hand man, made his way down the hallway, his deep frown obviously sending an unspoken message to Quentin.

Quentin took in the expression. "I've got a phone

call," he announced to no one in particular. To Kate he said, "Just tell the cook what you want."

"Something up?" Brody asked Quentin, his tone unconcerned, his body language casual and relaxed.

"Just puttin' out a fire. Nothing new."

"Can I help?" Brody asked.

Quentin looked puzzled by the offer, while Rex looked annoyed.

"Most of what messes us up in my organization are international issues," Brody said.

Quentin looked at Rex. "He does have international connections."

"Is this a Europe thing?" Brody asked.

"Let's talk," Quentin said, giving a nod toward the office.

As the three men moved away, Quentin turned back.

"Check out the gatehouse," he told Kate.

She didn't understand and must have looked confused.

"Take a look at Francie's jewelry. You're welcome to pick something. There'll still be plenty left for Annabelle."

Kate started to shake her head in protest. But she quickly stopped herself.

"That's very generous," she called out instead.

Brody smirked.

She knew what he was thinking. She didn't blame him. And it was what she wanted him to think anyway. She shouldn't feel so bad that her plan was working.

Five

Quentin's problem turned out to be mundane, which was disappointing for Brody. He didn't learn anything new about Beast Blue. There were some content issues with one of his games in the China market, and approvals were bogged down in red tape with a government agency. Brody had dealt with similar problems in the past and was able to give some advice on making it through the bureaucratic maze.

Brody wasn't wild about helping Beast Blue Designs make more money, but he did recognize the value of increasing his stature with Quentin. Rex was obviously annoyed that Brody got to play the hero. But then Rex was always annoyed about something. With respect to Quentin, Rex acted like a jealous lover.

Though it was only midmorning, Brody had had enough for one day. There were too many people around to take another run at Quentin's computer, and he didn't want to annoy Rex any more than necessary. The man might be obnoxious, but he was firmly in the inner circle of Beast Blue Designs. He might be valuable at some point.

On the way back down the driveway, Brody's attention caught on the gatehouse. He saw Kate though the window. The glimpse was fleeting, but it was enough to take him back to their kiss. That kiss had been amazing. It had all but short-circuited his brain and that never happened to him.

He repeated to himself that it wasn't something he could pursue, not here, and definitely not with someone like Kate. Forget about his problems with Beast Blue, she was nowhere near his type, nowhere near the kind of woman who normally attracted him. He acknowledged all that. He all but mentally shouted all that to himself. For all the good it did him, because his hormones didn't seem to care.

He found himself swinging into the parking space between the fence and a small patio. What the heck he was doing, he didn't want to guess.

A French door with glass panels was standing open, so he cut around the garden and poked his head into the modest foyer. Kate was at a small desk in the living area. A drawer was open, and she was working her way through a stack of papers.

"Looking for appraisal certificates?" he asked, attempting to open with a joke.

She jumped and turned guiltily at the sound of his voice.

Her reaction aroused his curiosity, and he took a few steps forward.

"Good guess," she said, with a nervous-sounding laugh.

He wasn't buying it. He'd caught her at something. He moved closer to get a look.

She quickly stuffed the papers back in the drawer and pushed it shut, turning to block it.

"What were those?" He made a show of looking around her.

"Nothing." She gave an airy wave of her hand. "A bunch of bills and stuff."

"Francie paid her own bills?"

Kate seemed to become even more flustered. "Well, not bills exactly."

"Are you looking for a will?"

"What? No."

He reached for the drawer.

"Are you allowed to do that?" she asked.

"Are you?" he challenged.

"Quentin told me I could look around."

"At her jewelry." Brody closed his fingers over the drawer handle.

She grabbed his wrist.

The contact startled him, but it didn't stop him. Although her cool fingers were distracting, she was absolutely no match for his strength. He slid the drawer open.

Inside, there were takeout menus and a couple of celebrity magazines. Kate's guilty reaction made absolutely no sense.

"Are you embarrassed to be interested in Trey Chatham's latest girlfriends?" he joked.

He pulled out the magazine to take a closer look. And then he saw it, a shallow, clear-topped jar of marijuana. Next to it were rolling papers and a lighter.

"Seriously?" he asked her.

A blush moved up her cheeks, but then she gave her streaked purple hair a defiant toss. "I wasn't going to smoke it."

"Of course not," he drawled.

"I was looking…" She seemed to have stumped herself. "I was just looking, okay?"

"It's eleven o'clock in the morning," he said.

"Thank you for that update."

"I'm saying it's a little early to get high."

"I'm not getting high. I don't do drugs. Don't make assumptions about me just because your rock-star friends indulge before noon."

"That wasn't why I was making the assumption."

She put her nose in the air. "Not that it's any of your business."

"You're young," he said.

He knew he shouldn't care one way or the other about what she did with her life. But she was fresh and vibrant. Since arriving in California, he'd seen what a few years of the hard-partying lifestyle did to most people. Kate could still choose a different path.

"I'm twenty-three," she said.

"Do you want to make thirty?"

"I am definitely planning to make thirty."

"Then stay away from Quentin. Sure, today it's marijuana and champagne. But tomorrow it'll be cocaine. Add to that a few dozen sexual partners, and you'll—"

"Excuse me?" She came to her feet, glaring daggers at him.

He looked her up and down, taking in the provocative dress, her rounded breasts and those long, lanky limbs. With that funky hair and heavy makeup, she all but screamed sex.

"You know nothing about my lifestyle." She seemed genuinely offended.

"*I* kissed you," he said, without knowing why he said it.

She was right. He knew nothing about her lifestyle.

He was making assumptions. But they were reasonable assumptions considering the evidence he had in front of him.

"You consider that a promiscuous lifestyle?"

"It was a really great kiss."

His answer seemed to give her pause.

"You want to do it again?" he asked, shamelessly taking advantage of the conversation. Against his better judgment, against anything remotely resembling judgment, his desire to repeat the experience was growing by the second.

"No, I don't want to do it again." She tilted her chin in the air. "I'm going to check out my sister's jewelry."

"You haven't looked at it yet?"

"No." She began walking toward the bedrooms.

He followed. "You've been here for more than an hour."

"And aren't you an old busybody. Can't you leave anything alone?"

"I've never been called a busybody before." He couldn't help but be amused by the archaic term.

"That's what you are."

"I have a perfectly ordinary sense of curiosity."

"Why are you following me?"

He realized it was a reasonable question. "With

all this talk, you've got me curious about Francie's jewelry collection."

"As we've established, it's really none of your business."

"At least I'm consistent."

They'd entered what had obviously been Francie's room.

Kate stilled in silence, her expression going neutral. He couldn't help but wonder at the impact on her, entering the last place her sister had lived.

He waited to see what she would do.

She just stood there, her eyes darting around, her nostrils slightly flared, while her fingers curled into her palms.

"Do you recognize anything?" he asked gently.

No matter what he might think of her, this had to be hard. She had his sympathy on a human level.

She shook her head. "I hadn't seen Francie in a very long time. Not since she stormed out on my mother seven years ago."

"It was bad?" he guessed.

"It was bad. She was eighteen. There was a lot of shouting. Not that the shouting was anything new. But that time she left and never came back."

"Did you try to find her?"

Kate shook her head. "I wouldn't have known the first place to look. We were very different people back then." Then she seemed to catch herself. "Two years later, I graduated high school and left LA."

"I'm sorry," he said, thinking about his own brother. He couldn't imagine his life without Blane.

Instead of responding, she crossed the room to a big maple dresser, opening what was obviously a jewelry box on the top.

She stared at the contents for a moment.

"Wow," she uttered, her tone reverent.

He moved up behind her to see what was there.

The box was six tiers of polished, patterned wood. Two earring trays opened up on each side, the walls of the compartments lined with white satin. Necklaces hung from two wings, and a ring compartment popped out on the front.

Crystal-clear and colored gems winked from gold and platinum settings. To his surprise, amidst the riches, Kate zeroed in on a delicate gold chain with a small, gold bird charm. She lifted it in her fingers.

"What's that?" he asked.

She dropped it, as if he'd startled her. "Nothing." She moved on to a pair of diamond earrings. "Do you suppose these are real?"

"They are if Quentin bought them." If Brody had learned anything about Quentin these past weeks, it was that he tossed money around like parade candy.

She fingered a large emerald-and-diamond pendant. Then she lifted a bracelet of gold-linked, square rubies, draping it over her wrist. "Annabelle is going to have everything, isn't she?"

"Everything money can buy," Brody agreed.

Quentin lavished luxury on those around him. He might be a criminal, but he wasn't selfish with his stolen wealth.

"There's more to life than money," said Kate.

"You won't get me to disagree with that."

"I grew up poor."

He thought of his family's thirty-five-room castle, his mother's diamond tiaras and the art collection in the grand hallway. He wanted to be honest. He couldn't be detailed, but he didn't have to lie. "I didn't."

She gave a nod, putting the bracelet back. "I wouldn't wish poverty on Annabelle."

"I doubt Annabelle will ever have to worry about money."

Even if Beast Blue lost everything on their new game, and even if they paid massive fines, Quentin would still be many times a millionaire. He and Annabelle would scrape by.

"Is that why you're here?" he asked Kate.

She looked guilty again. "What do you mean?"

"For the money. So you'll never have to be poor again."

She seemed to ponder the statement for a moment. "That would make sense, wouldn't it?"

"It would make perfect sense."

"Then yes. Yes, that's exactly why I'm here." She turned her attention back to the jewelry box. "I bet some of this stuff is really valuable."

"Are you for real?" he asked.

"What?"

"One minute you seem…I don't know, principled. And the next you're the material girl."

"It must be the recreational drugs."

"You said you didn't do drugs."

"It's not like I'm going to admit to anything illegal."

"So, you do take drugs?" He was very sorry to hear that.

She turned, holding a sapphire-and-diamond choker to her neck. "What do you think?"

It looked fantastic. It would look even better without the dress, better still without anything at all. Except the shoes. She should definitely keep the shoes.

"Are you going to wear it or sell it?" he asked.

She gave a giggle. "I haven't decided yet."

"Material girl," he muttered.

"This?" she asked, switching to an elaborate diamond pendant.

"You'd need a security guard with you if you're actually going to wear it."

"I know a couple of guys from the Ukraine," she responded without missing a beat.

"See?" said Brody. "You're quick."

"Quick at what?" She selected a pair of ruby drop earrings.

He stared at her.

She looked guilelessly back.

"Those would suit you," he said, instead of trying to figure her out.

"You think?" She removed her own earrings and settled the rubies into her ears.

He stood back. "You'd have to lose the purple hair."

Her hand went to her head. "You don't like my hair?"

He took a look in the jewelry box, selecting a pair of sapphire studs and a matching pendant. "These will go with your hair."

He watched while she tried them on, helping her with the clasp on the necklace.

"What do you think?"

He stepped back again.

She was perfect. Even with the crazy hair, she was undeniably elegant. The sapphire gems brought out the blue in her eyes. The jewels were neither too large nor too small.

"You need a ballroom around you," he said. "Chandelier light shining down, an orchestra playing, gold filigree, fine art and a gown of sky-blue silk swirling while you dance."

He was picturing the grand hall of Calder Castle. She would look good there.

"I've never danced in a ballroom."

"You should."

"Have you?"

"I have." He found himself holding out his arms. "It's really quite easy."

She didn't fight as he drew her into his embrace. He danced a few steps, and she easily followed.

"You've danced before," he noted.

"Everybody's danced before."

He twirled her in a spin then pulled her back into his embrace. She felt fantastic against him.

"Are you keeping them?" he asked, nodding to the earrings.

"Are they the most expensive?"

"I don't think so." He'd bet on the emeralds.

"Then no."

"So, you are going to sell them." He was disappointed.

"Sure I'm going to sell them. The odds of me having to pay rent are a whole lot higher than the odds of me dancing in a ballroom."

He lowered his voice, settling her closer. "And if I could come up with a ballroom?"

"You'd better come up with a wealthy prince to go along with it."

"Would a viscount do?"

"Sure," she answered brightly. "So long as he's rich."

Brody thought about his home again. "He is. Well, for the moment anyway."

They swayed in silence in the small room. He held her close, breathing her essence, feeling her lithe form shifting against him, musing that he had no desire to let her go.

"It's a nice fantasy," she said against his shoulder.

After a moment, he drew back to look into her pretty eyes. "It is." He touched her earlobe, the contact with her tender skin feeling intimate in a way that was arousing. "You should keep these."

She gave a sigh. "A good sister would do that."

"You're not a good sister?" He desperately wanted to kiss her. He wanted to kiss her over and over again.

It was hard to figure out exactly what was going on between them. But it was surprising and compelling all at once.

"I'm not a good anything," she said in a small voice "I'm a survivor, that's it, Brody."

The sound of his name made his chest contract. "We're all survivors."

Then, unable to stop himself, he slid his hand to

her neck, stroking the soft skin, drawing her gently toward his waiting mouth, every fiber of his being anticipating the kiss. But she suddenly clapped her hands on his shoulders, her body stiffening before she moved out of his arms.

She turned to the jewelry box. "What do you think?"

What had just happened? Why did she back off?

"About what?" he asked, struggling to get his emotional bearings.

"What's the most expensive thing in here? I don't want to be greedy, but I don't want to be stupid, either."

Her words were like a bucket of cold water. That's what had happened. He'd been a fool. He kept seeing things in her that weren't there. She was a party girl like all the rest, frivolous, superficial and self-gratifying.

"The emeralds," he said.

She took the earrings, along with a matching necklace and bracelet, wrapping them in her hand.

Disgusted, he turned and headed for the door.

She didn't immediately follow, and when he glanced over his shoulder, he saw her also pocket the little bird necklace before shutting the jewelry box.

Six

After Brody left the gatehouse, Kate had returned the emeralds to the jewelry box, keeping only the gold chickadee necklace. She'd given it to Francie fifteen years ago, back when they were a team, when they'd stood together in the chaos wrought by their mother. It had been around Francie's neck the day she'd walked out.

Kate then drove back to her room at the Vista Family Inn and indulged in a long nap. When she woke, she showered and changed into comfortable blue jeans and a cotton blouse, relieved to have all the makeup off her face for a while. Then she dialed Nadia.

"Tell me how it's going?" Nadia opened without preamble.

"I don't even know where to start," Kate said. So much had happened in the last couple of days. She decided to begin with the most important point. "I met Annabelle."

"That's fantastic."

"Quentin's totally bought my act. He thinks I'm after Francie's jewelry."

"That's brilliant."

"His idea, not mine. But I'll use it."

"Good for you. And well-acted."

"And there are a couple of bodyguards there who speak Ukrainian."

"Did you talk to them?" Nadia asked.

"They're not overly friendly," Kate said. "And I think it's better to keep a low profile. The fewer people I talk to, the less chance I have to screw up."

"If you did talk to them, I bet they'd be impressed."

"Right. You've been teasing me about my accent since I was eight. Besides, I'm giving them an especially wide berth."

"So, what did you find out about Quentin? Is he a decent father? Can you come home now? I got a notice from the condo association that they're redoing the roof."

"Quentin is a self-indulgent child. Is it going to cost us any money?"

"They're doing an estimate. And I guess that's

what you expected, wasn't it? He sure doesn't come across as a candidate for father of the year."

"I'm beginning to think…" Kate paused. She wasn't sure she was ready to complete the thought.

"What?"

"That I might have to try to get custody of Annabelle. Is that terrible? Do you think I'm jumping to conclusions?"

Concern came into Nadia's voice. "Is it that bad? You're not a conclusion jumper."

"The nanny seems great." Kate didn't know what would be going on if not for Christina. "But Quentin's lifestyle is positively frightening. And the people he has coming and going. They're drinking. They're smoking. I'm positive some of them do cocaine."

"So, he's a criminal? That might help in the custody battle."

"Maybe," Kate allowed. "I'm not sure how seriously they take rich people doing recreational drugs in LA."

"Yeah," Nadia said. "Nobody we know ever got arrested for it, and they weren't even rich."

"I don't know what to do."

"I guess that depends on how serious you are."

Kate wasn't following. "What do you mean serious?"

"I mean are you really ready to take on the responsibility for Annabelle's care twenty-four-seven? Because that's huge, and you have to be positive you're in a position to see it through."

Kate realized it was a fair question. "I think I'm positive."

"That's not positive."

"I am positive."

"You're not picking out wallpaper."

"I know that." Kate might not have started the week trying to get custody of a baby. But now that the problem had been laid bare in front of her, she knew she had no choice. "You know what happens if nobody steps up."

Both she and Nadia had had less than ideal upbringings. Annabelle was so sweet, so innocent. She had so much promise and potential. She deserved a good parent.

Nadia didn't answer right away. "I do," she said in a soft voice.

"It's not happening on my watch."

"You're right. You're completely right. And I'm in."

"You'd still be willing to live with me?" Kate's chest tightened with emotion.

Francie might have been her sister by blood, but Nadia was the sister of her heart. They'd been together through thick and thin since they were five years old. They now both taught grade school in

Seattle, and they'd bought a cheery, two-bedroom-plus-den condo nearby. For all intents and purposes, they'd created a family.

"There's a little girl who needs someone," Nadia said. "Neither of us is walking away. So, first off you need to find out what the grounds are for declaring someone an unfit parent. You're her aunt. Hopefully, that puts you next in line."

Mind completely made up, Kate spent most of the next day in the library, reading law books and checking legal websites, researching. Then, in preparation to visit Annabelle again in her Francie persona, she went to a secondhand store, finding a pair of skin-tight, cartoon patterned slacks and a black net crop top.

She found herself impatient to get things rolling, but she didn't want to seem pushy and alienate Quentin. So she waited one more night before donning the new outfit and heading back over to the mansion.

Luckily, the housekeeper who answered the door recognized her and let her straight in. It was ten in the morning on a Wednesday. She hoped Quentin would be at work and that Annabelle would be awake.

She checked the kitchen first, peeked at the patio and pool, and then headed toward the staircase that led up to the nursery. Partway along the hall, she heard Quentin's voice coming from the office.

"Back off," he shouted at someone. He sounded very angry.

Kate halted, wondering what she should do. The open office door was directly opposite the staircase, and she couldn't slip past it without risking being caught.

"How many times do I have to say it," he continued. "Forget Ceci. I'm not going there."

There was a silent pause, so she assumed he was on a phone call.

"No," he said sharply. "Because I'm not cut out for prison, that's why."

A wave of anxiety washed through her. She took a couple of reflexive steps backward. If Quentin caught her eavesdropping, he'd never trust her again.

"It's different," he stated emphatically. "With Ceci, we're talking a whole other level."

Suddenly, he appeared in the doorway, phone to his ear. His vision instantly zeroed in on Kate.

She pretended to be walking forward, moving swiftly, making her tone cheerful and oblivious. "Morning, Quentin." She pointed to the staircase. "I was going to stop by and see Annabelle."

His gaze narrowed, as if he was deciding whether or not to believe her.

"She wasn't in the kitchen. Does she nap midmorning?" Kate stopped in front of him, a guileless smile pasted on her face.

"Call you back," he growled into the phone.

Kate neutralized her expression. "Is this a bad time? I didn't mean to disturb you."

"Work," said Quentin, ending the call. "What did you need?"

Kate smiled breezily again. "I wanted to say howdy to Annabelle, maybe get a picture of her for my mom. I promised I would."

It was a flat-out lie. Chloe hadn't shown the slightest interest in Annabelle, except as a way to get to Quentin and his wealth.

He still seemed tense, causing Kate to wonder again about the seriousness of the phone call. He'd talked about prison, and Ceci again. Was he planning on something more than party drugs? She told herself to stop speculating in front of him, afraid her suspicions would show on her face. There'd be plenty of time to think it through later.

But was somebody pressuring him to sell drugs? Maybe Ceci was a new designer drug. Even as she considered the possibility, it seemed ludicrous. Billionaires didn't need to sell illegal drugs.

"Quentin?" A male voice sounded behind her.

She turned to see Rex coming toward them.

Rex gave her a wide, overly friendly smile. He'd

gotten more suggestive each time he'd seen her. He was way too touchy, too flirty, and he kept giving her lingering looks that seemed to say they shared a special secret.

He clearly considered himself a ladies' man, and he didn't catch on to any of the subtle hints she was sending that she wasn't interested. Either that or he was ignoring them.

"Morning, gorgeous." His gaze took a tour of her sexy top, tight pants and purple spike-heeled suede boots.

It occurred to her that she was partly to blame. Her looks and actions sure weren't warning him away. She wished she could have it both ways, keeping up the facade while keeping her distance, but she couldn't.

"Morning, Rex." She forced herself to smile back, masking her dislike.

He gave her a hug. It was too tight and too lengthy, but she gritted her teeth and played along.

Then he gave her a kiss on the cheek and drew back, squeezing her hands for good measure.

She resisted the urge to wipe the kiss away.

"I'm heading up to see Annabelle," she told him, making a move toward the stairs. "Nice to see you again." She looked at Quentin. "Thanks for this. I really appreciate your hospitality."

Quentin seemed to finally relax. "Brody said you took the emeralds."

Kate's hand went involuntarily to the chickadee necklace she'd put on that morning. Then she reminded herself to look thrilled about her new riches. "The emeralds are spectacular."

"You have good taste," said Quentin, considering her closely.

"And you are extraordinarily generous."

"So I've been told."

"Francie was lucky to have you."

Quentin greeted the observation with a knowing smirk. "Francie knew how to take care of herself."

Kate wasn't surprised to hear that, but she pretended to be oblivious to the undertone. "She was a good big sister."

Quentin's phone rang in his hand. He glanced at the number, and then looked past her to Rex, his expression irritated.

"I'll get out of your way," she said cheerfully, and quickly headed for the stairs.

More footsteps sounded in the hall, and a gruff, Ukrainian voice joined the conversation. The bodyguards were back.

"Take the call," one of them said in English.

Kate glanced fleetingly back to see that it was the tall bald one who had spoken. He met her gaze.

She looked instantly away and quickly trotted up the stairs.

She was relieved to find Annabelle awake, sitting in a padded plastic chair on the carpet, grinning and kicking happily. Christina was folding a basket of baby clothes.

She greeted Kate with a friendly smile. "Good morning."

"Am I disturbing you?" asked Kate, her gaze drawn to the baby.

"Not at all. She's in a very good mood."

"I can see that." Kate crossed the floor to Annabelle.

"She slept right through the night," said Christina.

"Aren't you the clever girl," Kate cooed.

"She finished all her cereal at breakfast."

"Is that a good thing?" Kate couldn't keep the smile off her face as she crouched down. "Hello, sweetheart." She gave Annabelle her index finger to squeeze.

"Bah, bah, bah, bah," said Annabelle.

"I've just introduced solid foods," said Christina. "She seems to love eating. I was thinking maybe pureed carrots next. Either that or peas." Then she paused. "I'm sorry. This is probably boring for you."

"Not at all. I want to hear everything." Kate hesitated. "Would it be okay to hold her?"

"Go ahead," Christina said softly. "It's nice for Annabelle to have family."

Kate put one hand behind Annabelle's back, and cradled her head, lifting her gently to her shoulder. She was wearing a stretchy red one-piece outfit with a yellow giraffe embroidered on the front. She was soft and warm, and she smelled sweet.

Her hands immediately tangled in Kate's hair and pulled.

"You get in the habit of pulling it back." Christina laughed, pointing to her own sensible ponytail.

"It's fine." Kate could comb it out later.

Then Annabelle's legs went stiff, her face screwed up, and a distinctive rumble emitted from her bottom.

"Oh, dear," said Christina.

"Don't worry," said Kate. "It's what babies do."

Christina quickly came over. "I'll deal with that."

Kate didn't want her time with Annabelle to end. "I can help. Or I can change her. I don't mind."

"So, you're experienced at this?" Christina looked relieved.

"Not exactly," said Kate. "Maybe you could talk me through it?"

"Aren't you the brave auntie," Christina teased.

"I'm not overly squeamish."

"That's a switch." Christina pointed to a white,

padded change table with diapers, wipes and creams laid out on a shelf.

"Quentin doesn't do diapers?" Somehow, that didn't shock Kate.

"Neither did Francie."

"How is that possible?" Kate couldn't say she was surprised to hear Francie didn't like diapers. But how could a mother avoid changing her own baby?

"She thought that's what nannies were for." Christina's expression sobered. "She didn't seem prepared for the day-to-day job of being a parent."

"I'm sorry," said Kate as she laid Annabelle gently down on the change table.

"There's nothing for you to be sorry for." Christina took a step back to give Kate some elbow room. "I have to admit, I'm interested to see how you do at this."

"Given my dysfunctional parenting genes?"

Christina laughed at the joke.

"My mother wasn't much of a mother, either. So, Francie came by it honestly." Kate located a long zipper on Annabelle's outfit.

She might not have done this before, but obviously the outer layer had to come off before she could get down to business. An odor was now wafting through the air, and she could only imagine Annabelle wouldn't be comfortable for long. Though, for the moment, the baby seemed perfectly happy, still grinning and kicking her feet.

"You don't have to take her arms out of the sleeves," Christina instructed. "Just push the rest out of the way. Undo the tapes. Be careful she doesn't turn over."

"I've got her." Kate held on to Annabelle's legs, lifting just enough to slide out the soiled diaper.

Christina handed her a wet wipe.

It was decidedly awkward, but Kate managed to get the baby's bottom cleaned.

"Here's a fresh one." Christina handed over a folded diaper. "Spread out the tapes, then slide it under."

Annabelle was wriggling in earnest now.

"She's hard to hold." Kate laughed.

"She loves being naked."

"I don't blame her." The diapers might be functional, but they are also bulky and constraining.

"You should see her in the bath. She's in heaven."

"I'd like that," said Kate as she wrapped the diaper around Annabelle's tummy. "I'd like that a lot."

"I bathe her before bed," said Christina.

Kate couldn't resist. Without even doing up the onesie, she lifted Annabelle back into her arms, cradling her close. "She's an angel."

Christina stroked the baby's hair. "She is that."

"Am I interrupting?" Brody's voice was distinct in the nursery doorway.

Kate turned, and his attention seemed arrested by the sight of Annabelle in her arms.

It took him a minute to speak. "She looks like you."

Kate reflexively glanced at the baby. "She looks like a baby."

"It's the blue eyes." He moved closer, seeming to consider Annabelle.

"Francie had blue eyes."

"Let me," said Christina, taking Annabelle from her arms and making a discreet exit into her own connected bedroom. She shut the door behind her.

Kate didn't want to give up Annabelle, and she was annoyed with Brody for interrupting her visit.

After Christina left, Brody was still considering her.

"What are you doing?" he asked.

She went on alert. "About what?"

"I keep tripping up against it." His gaze was far too astute, too penetrating. "You're up to something here."

"Are you hungry?" she asked, hoping to change the subject. "I'm hungry. Maybe some eggs Benedict?"

"It's got nothing to do with the emeralds, does it?" he asked.

"Or waffles. I could definitely go for some waffles."

He moved, starting to circle her.

"Brody, what are you—"

"It's Annabelle. You're here for Annabelle."

Kate's mouth went dry, and she swallowed trying to relieve it. "Sure." She pretended to misunderstand his point. "That's right. I thought I'd get a picture of her today."

"No." He shook his head. "I saw your expression when I walked in."

"I don't know what you're talking about. I had no expression."

He took in her outlandish slacks and the sexy top. "What's your plan?"

"I don't have a plan."

"You're lying."

"Brody."

"I saw Bert and Ernie down there."

She assumed he meant the bodyguard team. She was only too happy to let the subject change, but she was frightened by how much he'd already guessed.

"I'll make you a deal," he said, his expression turning calculated. "You report to me on what they say, and I'll pretend you're here after money."

"I am here after money."

"No, you're not. But I'm willing to pretend you are. So long as you help me in return. You do that, and your secret will be safe with me."

"I have no secret."

"Stop," he told her with quiet finality.

She quickly weighed the pros and cons, and realized further denial would get her nowhere. "Okay," she said. "I admit nothing. But I'll do what you want."

"You know, you don't have to admit something out loud for us both to know it's true."

She didn't bother to acknowledge his words. "They did say one thing this morning. It was Bert. And it was in English."

"Which one is Bert?"

"The tall guy. Which one is Bert to you?"

"Same one," said Brody. "What did he say?"

"Take the call. He told Quentin to take the call."

Brody's brow furrowed. "What call?"

"I don't know, but Quentin got another call a couple of days ago. He refused that one. And Bert didn't seem happy at the time."

"Do you know who called?"

"Someone named Kozak. Maybe he called back today."

"Why didn't you tell me?"

"Because I didn't know I was on your payroll."

"You're on the payroll now."

"So it seems. Are we done?" She wanted the conversation to end, and for Brody to be on his way.

But he didn't leave. Instead, he took her fingertips

gently in his, like he'd done before. And just like before, she felt a warmth travel all the way to her chest.

"You're not who you pretend to be," he said.

"Are you?" she asked in return.

She instantly knew she'd touched on something. There was a momentary flash in his eyes—shock, or maybe even fear.

But then his expression smoothed and he eased in close. "I'm a man who finds you attractive."

It was easy to see that this time it was Brody trying to throw her off the scent of something.

She wasn't falling for it. "What's going on, Brody?"

"I'm about to kiss you."

"You know that's not what I meant."

"Doesn't matter. I'm going to do it anyway."

"Brody—"

His kiss cut off her words.

His lips were warm and firm. Unlike the last kiss, there was nothing tentative about it. She didn't care. If it was possible, this kiss was even better. And in seconds she was kissing him back.

His free hand went to the small of her back, pulling her intimately against him as he tilted her head, deepening the kiss.

She knew she should push him away, and she promised she would in just a second, just a moment, just a few more minutes of paradise.

But when he was the one to draw back, it was all she could do to keep from whimpering at the loss.

"Admit you have a secret," he said.

She wanted to say no, but the word wouldn't form.

"Like I said, it's safe with me." He cupped her face with his palm. "I promise, it's safe with me."

He gave her a brief parting kiss, and then he was gone.

Seven

Brody told himself to stop obsessing about Kate. But it was harder to do now that he'd confirmed there was more to her than met the eye. Plus, she'd become part of his investigation, so he needed to think about her. It was only prudent for him to try to figure her out. It was a double-edged sword, because thinking about her forced him to admit just how attracted he was to her.

It was Friday, and everyone seemed to understand what that meant. There would definitely be another party. He knew she'd be there, trying to listen in on Bert and Ernie. She'd be wearing something sinful, sipping champagne, and men would flock to her by the dozens and make a play. It was all he could do not to toss them one by one into the pool.

It was still afternoon, and he'd ducked into Quentin's home office again to take another shot at his computer. Will thought there might be a secure link from the home computer to the Beast Blue servers. If there was, it could net them the evidence they needed.

He heard footfalls in the hallway and froze at the keyboard. Just then, his cell phone rang. He swore under his breath, quickly jumping up from the desk chair, cursing himself for forgetting to turn off the ringer.

He swiftly crossed the room, leaning nonchalantly against a wall and put his phone to his ear.

The office door banged open, revealing Bert and Ernie. Both had their sport jackets parted, hands on the firearms in their holsters.

"Hello?" Brody said into the phone, measuring his breathing and schooling his features.

"Brody?" It was his brother Blane.

"Hi." He was always careful not to use names. He didn't want to give out any hints to his true identity.

"What are you doing in here?" Bert demanded, accent thick, while Ernie did a sweep of the room.

Brody pointed to his phone, feigning impatience at the intrusion.

Ernie checked the windows and the closet.

"Brody?" Blane repeated.

"Yes," said Brody.

Blane coughed into the phone.

"Are you okay?"

"Getting better," said Blane. "Mother's got herself in a flap about the community ball."

Brody inwardly sighed. "Of course she has."

"I know you hate these things."

"Get out," Bert ordered Brody, pointing at the office door.

Ernie moved to the computer, and Brody forced himself not to watch him. He didn't want to telegraph his fear.

"Tell her I'll be there," he said to Blane.

"Will you?"

"I think so. I hope so." The ball was only two weeks away, so Brody really wasn't sure.

"Get out!" Bert repeated.

Brody levered himself slowly away from the wall.

Ernie was reaching for the mouse. If he brought the screen up, he'd see the computer had been turned on. It wouldn't take a genius to know it had been Brody.

Bert said something in Ukrainian, and Ernie looked swiftly up at him.

Ernie answered back.

"You know what'll happen if you don't show up," said Blane.

Brody knew his mother would be upset. But if

things didn't go well here, missing a ball would be the least of Brody's worries.

"I'll try," he promised his brother.

Bert stormed forward, and his meaty hand clamped around Brody's upper arm.

Brody shook him off, giving the man a glare as he moved toward the door.

"Gotta go," he said to Blane.

"Is everything all right?"

"It's fine."

"You sound upset…"

"Someone here is annoying me." Brody glared at the two security guards. Then he moderated his tone as he passed through the doorway. "It's no big deal. Can I call you later?"

"No need."

Ernie shouted something in Ukrainian behind him, and a chill went through Brody's chest.

"What was that?" asked Blane.

"Call you later." Brody quickly ended the call.

He turned, expecting to see their guns drawn and trained on him. But they were shouting at each other.

A second later, he sensed another presence. He looked to see Kate standing in the hall beside him. Her blue eyes were wide. She was dressed in black leather leggings and a tight pink tank top. Her heels were spiked, the ankle boots shiny black.

His brain flatlined.

"What happened?" she asked in a nervous voice.

He stepped in front of her, moving them both out of Bert and Ernie's line of vision. "What are they saying?" he whispered to her.

Her expression said she was concentrating.

He tried to be patient. "Can you understand?"

"Ceci again," she whispered back.

"What about her?"

Kate listened. "She's important. She's here. Bert wants to… It's not making sense."

"Did you get a last name?"

"No, but they're fighting about Quentin. Ernie wants to hurt him, and Bert wants to wait. Maybe Ceci is their sister?"

"Did they say that?"

"No. I'm guessing."

The voices stopped and Brody heard the men's footsteps.

He grasped her arm. "Let's go." He hustled her along the hallway, around the corner and into the kitchen.

She glanced back around the corner.

"Don't look," he hissed.

She suddenly shrank against his chest. "They're carrying guns."

"They're security guards."

"They have guns in this house with a baby."

"They'll protect her."

"I'm not so sure they're even protecting Quentin."

Brody was beginning to think the same thing, but he wasn't about to throw that possibility out on the table. "If they weren't doing their job, Quentin would fire them."

She didn't argue the point.

As the immediate danger passed, he became acutely aware of her body against his, his arm around the curve of her waist. Her tank top was slinky and clingy, the pants were smooth, so smooth against his thighs. Her hair smelled like rich vanilla. It would take nothing at all for him to slide his palms up to her breasts, turn her, kiss her, peel off any and all of those silly, sexy clothes.

He rasped a deep breath. He wanted very badly to sweep her into his arms and carry her off.

She pulled away, breaking the contact, peeping around the corner again.

He willed his heart to return to normal.

"I think they're leaving," she said.

He curled his hands into fists and ordered himself to get it under control. She was beyond complicated, and she was confusing on so many levels. His family's future hung in the balance, and he was letting lust rule his brain.

* * *

After the run-in with Quentin's bodyguards, Kate's instincts told her it was time to take action. She didn't trust Quentin, and she sure didn't trust Bert and Ernie. Quentin might be irresponsible, but Bert and Ernie seemed downright dangerous. Brody was a puzzle, for sure. It was clear he wasn't with Bert and Ernie. But it wasn't clear he was with Quentin, either.

Whose side was he on? And how many sides were there?

Later that evening, from her hotel room, she dialed Nadia.

"Hey," Nadia answered. She was breathing hard.

Since it was seven in the evening, Kate assumed she was out for a bike ride.

"Where are you?" Kate asked, sitting down on the bed.

"Coming through the university. Where are you?"

"In my motel room."

"What's up?"

"Are you sure you can talk?"

"It's fine. It's good. Talk away."

"Well…" Kate struggled to frame an opening. "Things keep getting stranger. And I'm worried. I'm really worried about Annabelle."

"What's Quentin done now?"

"It's not just Quentin. It's beyond just Quentin. It's everything."

"Define everything."

"To start with, there's this guy named Brody. He's figured out I'm interested in Annabelle." Kate hadn't yet worked out if Brody represented a danger to her ruse or not.

"Will he tell Quentin?"

"He said he'd keep it a secret if I'd spy for him."

There was a pause before Nadia spoke. "You may have to elaborate on that."

"Brody wants to know what the Ukrainians are saying."

"Why?"

"Because they're up to something. And they have guns. And they don't get along very well with Quentin."

"Hang on. I'm stopping."

"Don't stop."

"I'm stopping and sitting down." The bike clattered in the background. "Okay. What on earth?"

"Something tells me I should trust him."

"Brody, right? Not Quentin."

"Yes, Brody."

"Why would you trust him?"

"Because he hasn't blown my cover so far. And he

seems smart. And at least he's not armed, and he's not doing recreational drugs."

"Well, there's a resounding recommendation."

"I need to get Annabelle out of there. I'm starting to worry about waiting too long. It feels like things at the mansion are getting more tense by the day."

"Can you call the police?" Nadia asked.

"I don't have anything to report."

"The drugs?"

Kate pulled her legs up onto the bed. "I'm afraid it won't be enough. And it would tip my hand. And Quentin would probably refuse to let me see Annabelle again."

Nadia went silent.

"That's why I'm thinking about Brody," Kate said. "He wants my help, so he might help me in return."

"Who are Bert and Ernie?"

"The Ukrainians."

"They're named Bert and Ernie?"

"I don't know their real names. Those are nicknames. Do you think I should do it or not?"

"Trust Brody?"

"Yes." Kate's heart rate sped up as she gave the answer. She realized how badly she wanted to trust Brody. She felt completely alone in this. And she was growing frightened for Annabelle. She needed an ally, and she desperately hoped Brody was the guy.

"What do you want me to say?"

"I want you to tell me that my instincts are right."

"Well, to be honest—"

"Yes, please be honest. I need you to be honest," Kate said.

"Since it seems like he already knows a big part of it, you don't have a lot to lose, Kate."

"You're right. What he doesn't know, he'll probably figure out anyway."

The risk was low, or at least most of it was already in play. That was what Kate wanted to hear.

The Friday party was well underway, with a crowd of people out on the pool deck and others in the great room and the kitchen. She looked for Brody, but didn't find him. There was also no sign of Bert and Ernie.

She was about to do another loop when she caught sight of Christina heading for the front door. She moved for a better view, curious about where she might be going, and she saw Annabelle, wide awake, gazing over Christina's shoulder at the party all around them.

It was nearly ten o'clock. Surely Annabelle should be asleep by now.

Kate hurried to catch up. She made it onto the

porch as Christina was opening the back door of a silver sedan.

"Christina?"

Christina turned at the sound of her name.

Kate started down the stairs. "What are you doing?"

"We're going for a drive." Christina bent down to lay Annabelle in her car seat.

"Where?" asked Kate in astonishment. "Why? Now?"

Christina clicked the harness into place and tucked a blanket snugly around Annabelle.

She straightened. "She does okay falling asleep during the week. But on weekends the music gets pretty loud in there."

Annabelle couldn't sleep in her own room? Kate couldn't believe it. Or rather she could believe it, but she found it appalling.

"Have you talked to Quentin about the problem?" she asked.

Christina coughed out what sounded like a laugh. "Uh, no."

"You don't think he'd tone things down for his own daughter?"

"I don't think he'd stay still long enough to listen to the request." Christina seemed to realize what she'd said, and she snapped her mouth shut, worry coming into her expression.

"It's all right," said Kate. "I'm not going to say anything to him. I wish I could." She wished if she did say something it would have a hope of making some kind of positive difference.

"You must have guessed by now that he won't change his lifestyle for anyone or anything."

Kate struggled to control her anger. "How does he expect this to work?"

"He doesn't care how things work. He pays other people to make things work for him."

Kate silently acknowledged the truth in the statement. Quentin's development seemed to have been arrested in college. And he saw Annabelle more as a novelty than as a living human being.

"Where are you taking her?" Kate asked.

"Just out for a random drive. She likes the windy roads. They put her right to sleep."

"Doesn't she wake up when you come back?"

"We come back after the music stops."

"You drive around all night?" Kate couldn't believe it.

What about Christina? How did she get any sleep?

"We'll come back around three," said Christina.

"That's ridiculous."

Christina gave a shrug, shutting the car door. "That's reality."

Kate made a quick decision. "I'm coming with you."

She'd tried to find Brody, and she'd tried to find Bert and Ernie. Brody wasn't the only person who needed information. Kate needed it, too. And Christina might be able to give her something she could use against Quentin.

Christina took in Kate's formfitting black-and-silver cocktail dress. "I have to say, it looks like you had a whole lot more in mind than babysitting tonight."

Kate waved a dismissive hand. "I'm only trying to fit in."

"Fit in with the 'billionaires who want trophy wives' club?" Again, Christina looked regretful. "I'm sorry. I don't know why I keep speaking out of turn."

Kate laughed. "I'm not vying to be a trophy wife. But it's easy to see that's how it looks."

"You seem so down to earth. I keep forgetting you're one of them."

"I'm not one of them. I'm pretending to be one of them."

Christina looked doubtful, but didn't dispute Kate's assertion as she headed for the driver's seat.

Kate didn't bother waiting for permission. She hopped right in on the passenger side.

"You're serious about this?" Christina's hand hovered near the ignition.

"Completely serious."

"So, you're really not here trying to snag a rich guy?"

Kate was realizing that she had to start being honest with the people who could help her. It was the only way she'd succeed.

Christina seemed trustworthy. And she was in charge of Annabelle. Honesty seemed like the best path forward.

"I'm only here because of my niece," she said, just throwing it right out there before she could change her mind.

Christina glanced into the backseat, and all vestiges of friendliness vanished from her eyes. "What do you mean?"

"We might not have been close, but Francie was my sister. I owe it—"

"So, her inheritance," Christina said coldly.

"No." Kate quickly shook her head.

"I get it. You want to set yourself up to control Annabelle's money."

Annabelle began fussing.

"I don't know that Annabelle has any money."

Would Annabelle inherit money? It seemed like Quentin had gone to some trouble to protect all of his assets from Francie.

Christina was still frowning.

"That's not what I mean at all," Kate said.

"I should have known."

Annabelle's cries grew louder.

"You've got it wrong," Kate said. "Please, just go ahead and drive. Let her sleep. I'll explain."

Christina didn't look happy. But she did pull away from the curb.

It took Kate about half an hour to walk Christina through the family history, her job in Seattle, her recent arrival in LA, and her plan to imitate Francie as a party girl in order to check on Annabelle's welfare. She hesitated, but left out her ultimate decision to try to prove Quentin was an unfit father.

After Kate stopped talking, there were a few minutes of silence.

"That's really nice," said Christina, a slight quaver in her voice. "I'm so glad Annabelle has someone who cares about her."

Kate immediately felt guilty. She hadn't meant to sound self-righteous. "You've done a whole lot more for her than I have."

"A nanny's not the same as family."

Kate gave in to an urge to reach over and cover Christina's hand. "You were here. I wasn't."

Christina glanced over at her, eyes shiny in the passing streetlights. "You're here now."

"I'm trying."

Christina gave a little laugh. "I never would have guessed, not in a million years. I thought you were just like her."

"Then I'm a better actress than I expected." Kate couldn't help thinking about some of the exchanges between her and Brody. She knew she'd been convincing, but she hadn't been able to fool him. At least not for very long.

"What are you going to do now?" Christina asked.

"I'm figuring that out," Kate said as they passed by hedges, porch lights and manicured lawns through the Hollywood Hills. "I don't suppose you know anything about Brody Herrington."

Christina gave her a curious look. "He hasn't been around long."

"He seems different."

"I try to stay away from all of them," Christina said.

"Not the worst choice in the world."

"Do you like him?"

"What? No. That's not why I'm asking."

"He's a great-looking guy."

"There are lots of great-looking guys in the world."

"I've seen the way he looks at you."

"How do you mean?" Kate knew she shouldn't be asking, but she couldn't help herself.

"Like he wants to eat you for lunch."

"He does not."

"I think he has a lot of money. He wears expensive clothes."

"You can tell?"

"Poor people don't hire nannies. So I've had some experience with how the rich dress."

"I'd never know a designer suit."

"That's because you're not a gold digger."

"Neither are you," Kate told her.

"Oh, I'd take the gold in a heartbeat if it came with the right man."

Kate smiled. "There's your key. The right man."

"I guess I'd take him if he was poor, too. But Brody's not poor, and he's got a thing for you."

And they were back to Kate and Brody again—not the place Kate wanted to go. Protesting hadn't gotten her anywhere, so she turned it into a joke.

"Well, I've got a thing for Annabelle, so Brody's going to have to get in line."

Eight

Brody couldn't understand what had happened to Kate. She'd said she'd be here tonight, and he'd counted on it. Just when his opinion was starting to change, she pulled something like this.

Bert and Ernie had been huddled in a corner talking half the night. If she'd been here, if she'd showed up, it would have been a prime opportunity to gather more intel. He was holding up his end of the bargain. He was going to make sure she held up hers.

He headed down the front stairs of the mansion, deciding on his next move. And there she was, coming out of the passenger side of a car, looking super-sexy in a tight, short black-and-silver dress and a pair of high heels.

She'd been on a date? Seriously? Her love life couldn't go on hold for one day?

He strode for the car, prepared to confront her. Whoever she was dating could stand aside. The driver's door opened, and Brody braced himself. But the guy who stepped out was no guy at all. It was the nanny.

He was more confused than ever.

Before the issue could sort itself out in his mind, the nanny retrieved Annabelle from the backseat. Brody couldn't imagine where they had been at this time of night.

"You promised you'd be here," he said to Kate.

"I was here," she retorted. "You weren't."

"I've been here for hours." He lowered his voice. "And so have Bert and Ernie."

"Annabelle couldn't sleep."

Brody had no idea how to respond to that. "And…" he all but sputtered.

Annabelle started to fuss in the nanny's arms.

"We took her for a drive," Kate said.

"I should get her inside," said Christina.

"You were touring the neighborhood instead of being here?" He was trying to wrap his head around her thought processes.

"Thanks for your help," Christina said to Kate.

A look passed between the two women before the nanny hustled up the stairs.

"You want to tell me what that was all about?"

"My niece. The *baby*," Kate said. "Crying. Lots. And motion puts her to sleep."

"I'm not buying it."

"You know you have a suspicious mind?"

"That doesn't mean I'm wrong."

She went silent, an intense expression coming over her face. Everything he'd ever suspected about her intellect was there in front of him to see.

"Tell me what you're thinking," he said.

She made him wait a moment longer. "Is there somewhere we can talk?"

"Absolutely." Whatever she was thinking or doing, he wanted to know about it.

"Somewhere that's not here."

"My car." He pointed to his black Audi rental.

They were both silent as they walked. Then they slid into the leather seats and buckled up.

He pushed the starter button and moved the shifter. "Start talking."

It took her a minute or so to answer. "Not yet. I want to be able to see your eyes while I talk."

"This is starting to feel like some kind of a game." He wasn't interested in being jerked around for whatever reason she might have.

"I'm trying to decide if I can trust you, Brody."

"You can."

"You're going to have to let me be the judge of that."

He gave up. He was curious enough that he'd do it her way. "My hotel has a nice lounge."

"That'll work." She slumped back as the car started to move. She seemed distracted, gazing out the window as the streetlights flashed past.

They cleared the driveway, and he pulled the car onto the winding mountain road.

He told himself to be patient, but his interest was piqued. "If the lounge isn't private enough, we can go up to my suite."

"Sure," she answered distractedly.

"Kate?"

"Hmm?"

"What's going on inside your head?"

"What?"

"You just agreed to go up to my hotel suite."

She blinked at him. "Did I?"

"Are you planning to seduce me?" He knew that wasn't the case, but a man could hope.

"No."

"I'm sorry to hear that."

Her tone turned tart. "You can't be surprised."

He grinned. "There we go. Now you're back."

He picked up speed, and the route took them down to the beach at Santa Monica. In front of the hotel, Brody handed the keys off to the valet and swiftly rounded the car to open Kate's door.

He couldn't help admiring her shapely legs as she stepped out of the car.

She caught him staring. "We're not on a date."

"It feels like a date. It could be a date."

"This is serious, Brody."

"Fine." As he righted his gaze, he couldn't help but notice the little bird necklace dangling against her chest. He touched a finger to it. "I thought you'd decided on the emeralds."

He hadn't intended to call her on stealing the pretty necklace. But the fact that she'd taken it, along with so many other things about her had him more than a little confused. He wanted to see how she'd explain it away.

She glanced down. "I put the emeralds back."

"You did not."

They were worth a fortune, and she'd had Quentin's permission to take them. Kate might not be a fortune hunter, but she wasn't a fool.

"He said I could take one thing, and I wanted this instead," she said.

"Why?"

"Because I gave it to Francie for her birthday."

There was regret in Kate's eyes. "A long time ago. When things were better between us."

Now Brody felt like a prize jerk.

"Can we go inside?" she asked.

They crossed the lobby to the quiet lounge in the back and found an empty table with deep cushioned chairs and a candle flickering on the polished black surface.

"Drink?" he asked.

"I'll take a club soda."

Brody also ordered a beer for himself and debated whether he should apologize.

Before he could decide, she spoke. "I've come to the reluctant conclusion that I'm going to have to trust you."

"Reluctant?" It was hard to take that as a vote of confidence."

"Look at it from my side, Brody. I don't know anything about you, or your relationship to Quentin, or what's going on with Bert and Ernie."

"But you need something from me." That much was clear.

She toyed with one of her dangling earrings. "I need to tell you that I'm a fraud."

"You're a criminal?" He certainly didn't want that to be the case.

"No." She pointed to her hair and her dress and her fingernails. "I mean I'm not this."

He wasn't following. Was she saying she wasn't Francie's sister? He hadn't even considered that as a possibility.

"I'm not like Francie. I don't like parties and loud music, and I certainly don't do recreational drugs."

"But you are her sister?"

His question seemed to confuse her.

"Of course I'm her sister. Who else would I be?"

Brody didn't know. But he was through taking anything at face value.

"What about the marijuana in the gatehouse?" he asked.

"You walked in just as I found it. I was putting it back."

"Okay."

She squared her shoulders. "Do you believe me?"

"Yes." He did. He hadn't seen anything else that indicated she was into any kind of drugs. When he thought back about it, she barely ever drank the champagne she ordered.

"I'm a first-grade teacher," she said.

"Really?" That wouldn't have even been his hundredth guess.

"I'm giving you the truth here. And I can prove it all. I cut my hair. It's not usually purple. I don't wear this amount of makeup, and my closet is full of ordinary dresses and blazers."

He found himself smiling. "So, I'm assuming this was part of some master plan?"

"I wanted Quentin to like me. I wanted to blend in. I wanted a chance to make sure Annabelle was being properly cared for."

What she said seemed to pull a lot of the pieces together, and Brody couldn't help but admire her ingenuity. "Well, you pulled it off. And you managed to look good doing it."

"I look tacky doing it."

"But sexy. Tacky can be very sexy."

"Stop."

"It's hard to stop when you're sitting right here in front of me."

"Be serious, Brody."

The waiter arrived and set down their drinks.

Brody waited until he left. "I am serious. But this is hardly the most damning secret in the world. You did a good thing."

"That's not all of it." She twirled the plastic stick in her icy drink.

She had his attention.

"I need someone close to Quentin to help me."

Brody almost told her he wasn't close to Quentin. But he didn't want to stop the flow of information. And he didn't want to disappoint her before he had to.

"I know he does illegal drugs," she said. "And I can probably get proof of that."

"I don't think that's a good idea, Kate, it would be dangerous for you to try."

"Even if I was successful, I don't think that's going to be enough."

"Enough to what?"

"To prove he's an unfit parent. I've been reading up, and it's not going to be enough to show I'd be a better parent. There has to be something significant to get her away from him."

Brody couldn't help but see the irony in the situation. If his own plans came together, Quentin wouldn't be in a position to raise Annabelle or any other child for a very long time to come.

She continued in the face of his silence. "Francie and I didn't have it very good growing up. Our mother was a narcissist and an alcoholic who didn't particularly like children."

"That sounds bad."

"It was bad. Maybe worse for Francie than it was for me. She reacted one way to the disaster that was our childhood. I reacted in another. Thing is, I survived. I'm doing really well in Seattle. I've got a great job. Great friends. I own a condo—well, half a condo. I fought hard and I climbed out of a truly dismal start in life. I'm in a position to take care of Annabelle. She doesn't have to be stuck with Quentin. The cycle doesn't have to repeat with her, because I can stop it."

Brody couldn't help comparing Kate's upbringing with his own. And he couldn't help picturing Annabelle. She was a beautiful little baby, cherubic, happy, curious. And she had Kate's blue eyes.

He didn't care that they were also Francie's blue eyes. As far as he was concerned, they belonged to Kate. And for some reason that told him Annabelle should be with Kate. And he wanted to help.

He knew the safe thing to do was keep quiet about his family. But he found he didn't want to play it safe. He wanted to go out on a limb for her. And that meant sharing more than he should. But she'd trusted him and, like him, she was trying to do the right thing by her family.

"I don't mean this the way it sounds," he said. "But would you come up to my hotel room?"

"How do you think it sounds?"

"Like I'm making a pass at you."

"But you're not."

"No. There's something I want to talk to you about, and I can't do it here."

It looked like she was fighting a smile. "'Come up to my hotel room, baby, and I'll tell you a secret'."

"If I was making a pass at you, it would be a lot smoother than that."

"I'm not judging."

"You were mocking."

"I guess I'm just relieved that now you know the truth about me and why I'm here."

He reached forward and took her hands. "That wasn't such a terrible secret. What you're doing is admirable. And if you'll trust me a little further, I have an idea."

"I trust you." She paused. "I guess in part because I have to. You're the only one of Quentin's friends who doesn't make the hair stand up on the back of my neck."

"Your instincts are good. You should keep going with those."

Kate was drawn to the glass doors that led to the balcony of Brody's hotel suite. He had a sweeping view of the ocean and stars, and a quarter moon that hung low in the sky, and she gazed out at the panorama.

"Open?" he asked, coming up beside her.

"That would be nice."

It was coming up on three in the morning. Her energy was waning, but as he pulled aside the doors the ocean air blew in, reviving her.

"Thirsty?" he asked.

"I'm fine."

"Would you like to sit?" he asked, gesturing to the sofa.

"You're making me nervous," she said.

"Don't be."

If only it were that easy. She wasn't completely sure she was ready for whatever he had to say that was so private. She hoped it was something good about Annabelle.

He took the opposite end of the sofa, then he seemed to hesitate. "Right. Here it is."

She waited.

"Here's what?" she asked, her curiosity beginning to turn into anxiety. Was it something bad?

He gave a tight smile then pressed his lips together. "My name is not Brody Herrington."

A warning tingle flooded Kate's body.

"What?"

"I'm not—"

She came to her feet, the hair on the back of her neck standing on end. Why had it seemed safe to come up here with him? She didn't even know him. She didn't know him at all.

"Wait," he said.

She turned to leave, and he jumped up from the sofa.

"It's Brody Calder," he called after her. "Kate, stop. It's nothing sinister, I promise."

Her hand was gripping the door handle. She didn't let go, but she stared at him cautiously.

"I'm Brody Calder. My grandmother's name is Herrington. My family and I own Shetland Technology Corporation. It's a Scottish firm that's a direct competitor of Beast Blue Designs."

She tried to wrap her head around what he was saying. "You're not a concert promoter."

That much was clear.

"I'm not."

"So you're some corporate spy? You're a criminal? Are Bert and Ernie the good guys?"

"No! And I'm not a criminal. And Bert and Ernie are definitely not the good guys. My family and I are the victims. Quentin stole from us, and I'm here to prove it."

"What did he steal?" She couldn't imagine what Quentin would want that he couldn't buy for himself.

"Intellectual property. Computer code."

Her instincts were at war with themselves, some telling her to get away from Brody, the rest telling her to trust him. "Why should I believe you?"

"Because you've met Quentin, and you've met me. Which one of us do you think is a thief?"

"There's no way to know."

"There are dozens of ways to know."

"Name one." She kept a firm grip on the door handle.

If he made a single move toward her, she was running out into the hall and shouting for help.

"Do a search on me. Use my real name. You'll find my family, and you'll find my company. You'll know I'm telling the truth about that much."

"You'll stay where you are?" she asked.

"Absolutely." He sat back down and held up his palms in mock surrender. "Go ahead."

She took out her phone and pulled up the browser. "You said Calder."

"Yes. Try the Earl of Calder. My father."

She studied his expression. "Is this a joke? Some kind of con?"

"You're about to find out."

She typed.

The photo was small, but it was clearly Brody. He was the second son of the Earl of Calder. She let go of the door handle, somewhat relieved.

"You can use my computer to look further," he offered.

She glanced up. "You're a viscount?"

"My older brother, Blane, is a viscount. When my father dies, Blane will be Earl. That's how it works."

"But you're the son of an earl."

"Guilty."

She was thoroughly confused. "What are you doing? Why are you here? You're taking a huge risk. Why not just call the police?"

"That was the first thing I tried," he said, looking suddenly tired. "On both sides of the Atlantic."

She moved back toward the sofa, her fear dissipating. She found she believed him. "This is a lot to take in."

"I understand that."

She studied him, wondering if there was something she should have seen, something that should have stood out, setting him apart from the rest. Then she realized there was. She'd come to him for a reason. Of everyone near Quentin and Annabelle, Brody was the one she'd innately trusted.

When she looked at him now, his honesty, his intelligence and his integrity shone through.

She sat down. "Quentin is a thief."

"He is."

Her mind cataloged the implications and the possibilities. "And you're trying to prove it, to get him fairly and justly charged, convicted and maybe sent to jail."

"I am."

"Okay." She nodded. "Okay. I'm in. What do we do?"

Brody smiled. "Thank you."

"You don't have to thank me. This is for Annabelle. I should be thanking you." If Brody was right, and if they could prove it, she'd have more than a fighting chance with Annabelle.

"We think there might be proof on Quentin's home computer."

"Who is we?"

"My head programmer, Will Finlay, and me."

"So that's what you were doing the day you said we were looking for your watch." She saw all of his actions through a whole new lens.

"Again, guilty. There was never any watch."

"You kissed me to throw me off." Her mind went back to the moment.

"I kissed you because I wanted to kiss you. But I'd have done it again then to keep Bert and Ernie off the scent." He paused. "Heck, I'd have done it again then or any other time, and with any excuse, or with no excuse at all."

The atmosphere shifted, their kisses thrown out front and center. The air seemed to warm, and the room seemed to shrink around them.

"I knew you never quite fit," he said, and he shifted across the sofa towards her. "You were crazy and sane, smart and scattered. Your ridiculous clothes and outlandish hair never meshed with your core personality. The real you kept slipping through."

"I kept wanting to trust you," she said.

"I'm an honorable man."

"Is that a viscount thing?"

He reached up and slowly cradled her cheek. "That's my brother's title."

She liked the feel of his hand. She loved his closeness. She was so relieved that they were being honest with each other.

"You were conning me while I was conning you."

"I don't know who won that round." He touched his forehead to hers.

"Call it a draw."

"Sure. But in honor of our new spirit of honesty and full disclosure. Fair warning. In about three seconds I'm going to kiss you."

"I think…" She tipped her head for his kiss. "It's good to be on the same side."

"I think so, too."

His lips claimed hers, tender at first but then with a deepening passion and a hardening purpose. She wrapped her arms around his neck, molding her breasts to his body, giving in to the desire she'd been fighting for days.

He was sturdy and strong, an anchor point she desperately needed. She opened to him, and their kiss went on and on, sexy and impatient, probing and exhilarating.

His hand slid to the small of her back, splaying over her spine. He shifted her to his lap, his slacks arousing friction against the backs of her bare legs.

His lips moved to her neck, planting hot, moist kisses in the sensitive hollows. He pushed a strap of her dress from her shoulder, kissing his way to the tip. Her nipples hardened and tingled, aching for his touch.

He read her mind, and he cupped her breast.

She moaned his name, arching her back, sighing with pleasure as he pushed her dress down. It pooled at her waist.

"You are incredible," he whispered, then he kissed a path from her neck to her breasts.

She all but melted in his arms, letting the pleasure wash over her.

Her dress rode up, and his thumb brushed the lace of her panties.

"I want you," he said on a rasp. "All of you. Every inch…"

"I want you, too," she managed to say. "Now."

She'd never been so brazen, but she had no intention of stopping him.

He stripped off her panties in one deft motion.

Her body contracted with intense sensations, the cool air, his hot touch, his kisses that went on and on, along her neck, up to her mouth.

Her lips were swollen and burning and eager for more. She turned in his lap, facing him, straddling him, gripping his shoulders tightly. She had no desire to control the wild passion building between them. For now, for a moment, in this tiny space and time, nothing existed but Brody.

She plucked at his shirt buttons, releasing them one by one. Then she pulled the sides open and pushed his sleeves down. His shoulders were magnificent, smooth, toned and tanned. She kissed one of them, tasting his skin, smelling his skin.

He stripped off his shirt, wrapping his strong arms around her, pressing them together. The heat of his chest fanned the pulse in her core. She reached for his pants, releasing the zipper. He helped, raising her up, freeing himself, then splaying her hips with his hands and bringing them together as one.

She gasped, staring into his eyes. "That is…"

"You're amazing," he whispered as he started to move.

"Oh, Brody."

"I know."

Pleasure and joy pulsated through her. She rocked her hips in time with his. She held on to his shoulders, tighter and tighter. She kissed him again, their tongues tangling, deeper and deeper still.

The world disappeared. Her whole body was alive, alight with the buzz of pleasure. She turned hot and then cold and then hot again.

He trailed his fingers on the curve of her breast, circling in, closer and closer until he reached the center.

She cried out, bucking against him, striving desperately to close any last space between them.

He wrapped her in his arms. Then he turned her, pressing her back onto the sofa, stretching them chest to chest, thigh to thigh, toe to toe. He linked their hands, raising them over her head.

Then he watched her. He held her gaze, and she felt like she was falling headlong into his polished-pewter eyes. His strokes were taking her to heaven, and she let it come. She lay still. She absorbed his pace. She let him into her body, her mind and her soul.

The pulses of pleasure came faster and harder, as she soared to an unbearable height.

"Kate!" he cried out.

His body shuddered around her, and she catapulted to the edge of oblivion.

She couldn't see. She couldn't hear. She couldn't move.

She was floating, blissfully.

"Kate?" His voice was a long way off.

"Hmmm?" She wasn't capable of forming actual words.

"You are the most incredible woman I've ever met."

She smiled. Then she opened her eyes. He was blurry in front of her.

"You're very good at this," she said.

"I'm not that good." He kissed her shoulder. "I'm not this good. I think it must be you."

"I'm not that good, either." She had never had sex that came close to this experience.

"Then it must be us."

"I bet it was the relief."

Now that it was over, she could take a step back and analyze her intense feelings for Brody.

"The relief?"

"You're going to help me with Quentin, with Annabelle. It's a huge relief to have someone on my side."

"And that translates into mind-blowing sex?"

"It seemed to."

"Because, Kate." He looked completely genuine. "I

don't know what sex is like where you come from, but that was off the charts."

She knew what he meant, but she wanted to keep it light. "You don't have sex that good in Scotland?"

"Man, I'm going to have to visit Seattle."

Kate grinned.

He captured her hand and kissed her fingers. Then he smoothed back her hair, his voice going lower. "You have rocked my world."

She gave in to honesty. "You rocked mine, too."

He wrapped her in another tight hug.

The last thing she wanted to do was break the spell. But they were running out of night, and their problems would still be there in the morning.

"But right now," she said. "We need to talk about Quentin."

He heaved an exaggerated sigh. "I know."

Brody rose, and she watched him stride naked to the bathroom. He emerged a few minutes later with two fluffy robes and dropped one beside her.

"You know this moment could be truly sublime," he said, shrugging into the other. "We could order some room service, feed each other truffles and champagne, talk about our hopes and dreams and plans for the future."

She sat up and put on the robe, grateful for the

warmth. "Our plans for the future are to annihilate Quentin."

"And that hardly lends itself to afterglow, does it?" He sat next to her.

"Buck up, Brody." She gave him a playful elbow. "Tell me how I can help."

"Aren't you the no-nonsense schoolteacher."

"If I can keep twenty first graders in line, I can handle one almost-viscount. What should I do?"

He sat back, a serious expression coming over his face. "The best thing you can do is spy on Bert and Ernie."

"I really don't like those guys."

"Like I said, your instincts are good."

"Is there a reason you think they know something?"

"They're not your run-of-the-mill bodyguards. If I was running a criminal enterprise, those are the guys I'd want on my team."

"Do they seem like overkill to you?" she asked.

"That's a good question." Brody seemed to consider the point. "If all Quentin did was steal our computer code, why does he need those guys? He needs techies to incorporate the code into his game. And he needs a sales staff to get it to market. But why those two running around his house all the time?"

"Maybe he's stealing something else."

"It's possible." Brody looked unconvinced. "Even if he is, in Quentin's world, you need nerds for thieves, not thugs."

"I'll do my best to find out."

Kate might prefer to stay away from Bert and Ernie, but she agreed with Brody's assessment. And she was grateful for his help. Her chances of helping Annabelle had now drastically improved, and it was thanks to Brody.

Nine

Kate and Brody slept for a couple of hours, and then she returned to the mansion to execute their new plan.

It was quiet there, with no sign of Christina and Annabelle on the main floor. So Kate made her way up the staircase. Near the top, she heard Annabelle crying.

The crying grew louder. She found herself hurrying, pushing open the nursery door, wondering what could be wrong.

She was surprised to find Annabelle alone. As she rushed to pick her up, a figure on the floor caught the corner of her eye.

"Christina?" she said out loud as she scooped Annabelle from her crib.

The baby's eyes were swollen, her face red, her nose running. Kate cradled her against her shoulder as she rushed to Christina's side. She was unconscious, lying motionless, her face pale, her hair streaked with sweat. Her forehead was hot to the touch.

"Christina?" Kate tried again, juggling Annabelle and reaching into her pocket for her phone.

Christina's eyes blinked open. They were glassy and confused.

"Are you okay?" Kate asked, even though it was obvious she was not. "I'm calling for an ambulance."

"Annabelle," Christina croaked out.

"I've got her," said Kate. "She's upset, but she's fine."

Christina tried to sit up.

"Don't," ordered Kate.

"She's hungry."

"I'll get her a bottle." Kate pressed 911.

"Fire, police or ambulance?" came the immediate response on the line.

"Ambulance," said Kate, and she gave them the address.

"You need to feed her," Christina mumbled weakly.

"I will."

Footsteps sounded in the hallway.

"Help," Kate called out.

The footsteps stopped, and Rex was in the doorway. When he took in the scene, his jaunty, expectant smile was gone.

"I've called an ambulance," said Kate. "Christina's burning up, and Annabelle needs a bottle."

"I'll get someone to help," said Rex.

He disappeared, and almost immediately one of the housekeepers entered the nursery.

"I'll stay here, miss, and someone will meet the ambulance downstairs," the woman said.

"Thank you," Kate said to the housekeeper. "I'll get Annabelle a bottle." Kate gave Christina's hand a squeeze, but Christina seemed oblivious.

Kate juggled Annabelle as she walked, shushing her and promising food was on its way.

She'd watched Christina prepare bottles, so she knew where everything was kept, how to heat up the formula, and to test the temperature on her wrist. She also knew how to hold Annabelle. It was a bit awkward, but between the two of them, they got it sorted out, and Annabelle settled down.

She heard the ambulance arrive, and people going up and down the stairs. She was grateful that Christina was going to be in good hands. After a while, the noise subsided, and Rex came into the kitchen.

"How is she?" Kate asked him.

"They took her away."

It wasn't exactly an answer, but she supposed that was all she was going to get. She hoped it was nothing serious. She'd come to like Christina very much.

"How are you doing?" Rex asked, moving closer to her.

Kate felt her guard going up. His tone was solicitous, but there was something about him that always seemed calculating and cunning. He tried to flirt with her whenever he got the chance. So far, she hadn't responded with any encouragement. Yet he persisted.

"We're fine." She had to struggle not to feel intimidated. "I mean, Annabelle's fine. She's the only one we need to worry about."

His glance went fleetingly to Annabelle. "I assume that smell is her?"

"I decided hunger was more pressing than a fresh diaper."

Rex wrinkled his nose. "I'm not sure you made the right choice."

"That's only because she's quiet. If she was still crying, you'd agree with me."

"Maybe," he said.

His gaze on her was distracting, and it made her want to shift in her seat. She wished he would back up a bit. As it was, with her sitting, it felt like he was looming over her.

"Is Quentin up?" she asked, instinct telling her to remind him there were other people in the house.

"Not that I've seen."

"He must have heard the ambulance."

Rex gave a shrug. "He's a sound sleeper."

He awkwardly wriggled Annabelle's foot, and it was all Kate could do not to slap his hand away. She didn't want him touching the baby.

"So, tell me, Kate," he said. "How are you enjoying LA?"

"I grew up in LA."

"Not in a place like this."

She found herself glancing at the surroundings. "No, not in a place like this."

"You like it?"

"What's not to like?" She tried to figure out where he was going with this conversation. Surely, after all the worry and concern only minutes ago, it wasn't the time now for chitchat.

He sat down in the chair next to her at the table.

She resisted an urge to scoot back.

"How long are you planning to stay?" He rested his hand on the tabletop.

"I don't know. I haven't given it much thought."

Rex was plummeting along with Bert and Ernie on her trust meter. She didn't know how he might factor in to Quentin's crimes, but she definitely didn't like being alone with him.

"Oh, I suspect you've given it some thought." He moved his hand closer to her.

Her grip tightened on Annabelle, and the baby squirmed. Kate forced herself to relax.

She pretended to misinterpret his question. "I can take care of Annabelle as long as Christina's sick."

"Is that what this is about?" He brushed the back of his knuckles against her forearm. "Annabelle."

Kate didn't like him getting anywhere close to the truth. She subtly pulled away from his touch. "She is my niece."

"You don't strike me as the maternal type."

"I'm not." She told herself to think like Francie again. Her sister wouldn't have been intimidated by Rex. "I'm the cool-auntie type. I plan to take her shopping and stuff."

"With Quentin's money?"

"He is her father."

Brody barged full force into the kitchen, his gaze immediately locking on Kate. "What was with the ambulance?"

She was incredibly grateful to see him.

Rex gave him a glare. "Look who's still hanging around."

"Christina is sick," she said, adjusting Annabelle in her arms. "Everything else is fine."

"What kind of sick?" Brody asked.

"A fever, maybe only a flu or something. But she had passed out when I found her."

"Are you all right?"

Rex came to his feet. "Does she look like she's not all right?"

"I'm fine," Kate said.

Annabelle's suckling was slowing down, so Kate removed the bottle and raised her to her shoulder to burp her.

"She needs a change." Kate was glad for the excuse to get out of the conversation.

"What are you doing here?" Rex asked Brody.

"I came to see Quentin."

"Quentin won't be up for hours."

"I'm up now," came Quentin's voice as he sauntered into the room. "What's going on?"

Kate jumped in before anyone else had the chance. "Christina's sick. So I'm taking care of Annabelle."

Quentin seemed to digest that for a moment.

She held her breath and waited. She wanted all the time she could get with Annabelle, and the more she hung around, the more opportunities she'd have to eavesdrop on Bert and Ernie. Not to mention Rex. She was starting to get suspicious of Rex.

"Oh," was all Quentin said.

She let go an inward sigh of relief, taking his lack of interest as permission to stay.

Brody gave her a subtle look of approval.

"Welcome aboard," said Rex, a mocking edge to his tone and a predatory glint in his eyes.

She was definitely going to have to be careful around him.

"Annabelle needs a change," she announced.

Quentin inhaled and scowled. "You're telling me."

Kate hopped to her feet and headed for the hallway.

Brody stopped her with a gentle hand on her arm. His touch had a ripple effect across her body.

"You sure you're okay?" he asked in an undertone.

"It's all good," she said.

Rex broke in. "What's with the whispering?" he asked them.

She pulled her arm free. "Brody's offering to change the baby."

Brody made a show of surrender. "I'll pick up formula, shake a rattle or move the car seat. But you're on your own for the sticky stuff."

"I guess I misunderstood," she quickly told Quentin, adding a giggle for good measure.

Rex seemed to be getting far too suspicious. She and Brody were going to have to be careful to keep up their charades.

She gave Quentin a smile and thought airy Francie thoughts.

She held Annabelle up like an accessory. "I thought
we'd go to the mall. I could pick us out matching
outfits and get our picture taken. Or maybe I should
get her ears pierced. She'd look darling, don't you
think?"

Before anyone could react to the outrageous statement, she breezed from the room.

The next day Brody watched Rex head up the main
staircase. He knew where the man was going and
he didn't like it. Kate had moved into the mansion
yesterday, taking Christina's room, since it was connected to the nursery. Moving in was a good move
from the perspective of spying, but now Rex was
stalking her.

Brody took the stairs two at a time.

"Soundproof?" Rex was asking as Brody rounded
the corner into the nursery.

"Sound dampening, anyway," said Kate.

She was on the floor, a cutting tool in her hand, colorful rolls of material and cardboard cartons strewn
around the room. Annabelle was cooing in the crib
which had been pulled away from the wall. All of the
furniture was moved toward the center of the room.

"What are you doing?" Brody couldn't help but ask.

Redecorating seemed like an odd choice given their current plan of trying to have Quentin arrested. Then again, he supposed Quentin wouldn't suspect she wanted to take Annabelle away if she was nesting in the nursery. If that was the plan, it was pretty good.

Rex gave Brody an annoyed frown. It was clear he wanted Kate all to himself. Too bad, because Brody wasn't going anywhere.

"Quentin told me I could make a few changes."

She was dressed in worn jeans, a plain red T-shirt and a pair of runners. Brody was sure this was the first time he'd seen her without makeup. Except for the purple hair, she looked like the perfect girl next door.

He found the look very sexy. Truth was, he found all of her looks sexy. This was just another in a long list.

"Wallpaper?" he asked.

There had to be easier means to accomplish the same objective.

"It has a sound barrier on the inside." She pointed to the quarter-inch material. "And on the outside, well, you can see the pretty trees and birds."

Brody wasn't sure he followed her complete logic. But he was willing to go along with it.

"You're going to need help with that," he said.

If Rex stayed, Brody stayed.

"That would be great." She gave him a grateful smile as she came to her feet, retrieving a measuring tape.

He had to admire her acting. Rex thought she was planning to freeload. Quentin likely did, as well. It was good to feed into their mistakes. It would keep them from thinking about other possibilities.

"I'll give you a hand, too," said Rex, rolling up his shirtsleeves.

No surprise there.

"Thanks," Kate said.

Brody knew she was no fan of Rex, so he applauded her acting once again. Then he rolled up his sleeves, as well. He was far from a home decorating expert. But if she was determined to do this, he could provide brute strength.

Annabelle's vocalizations grew louder, as if she wanted to participate in the conversation. She rolled from her back to her stomach, blinking at them.

As always, he was struck by her eyes—Kate's blue eyes. Her cheeks were plump and rosy pink, and she had a soft halo of light hair. For a moment, Brody thought of his mother and her intense desire for grandchildren. She was anxious for an heir, and his parents were pushing his brother, Blane, to get married.

He suspected it was more than just the need for an heir to the earldom. His mother had a soft spot for both babies and children. Her charitable work focused on children, and there was nobody more enthusiastic about the annual summer children's festival that took place on the grounds of the Calder estate.

"The directions say to start with plumb lines," said Kate.

Annabelle picked that moment to cry out. Her little face screwed up, she quickly began to wail.

Kate glanced at her with worry, her hands already full. "Oh, baby. Does it have to be right now?"

Brody impulsively stepped forward. "I'll get her."

Kate looked surprised by the offer. "Are you sure?"

"I'm sure."

"Do you know what you're doing?"

He frowned at her. But it was true that her instincts were bang on. He'd never held a baby before. Not that he was about to admit it. It couldn't be too complicated. Annabelle was soft, warm and fragrant.

His confidence faltered. She was a little too fragrant, and not in a good way.

She gulped down a sob, eyeing him with surprise and trepidation.

"Hey there, Annabelle," he said softly, giving her

what he hoped was a reassuring smile. "Something bothering you?"

She sniffed a couple of times, clearly deciding whether or not to keep crying.

"Your auntie's busy right now," he crooned.

He could hear Rex guffaw in the background, but he ignored him. Rex might be too macho to take care of a baby, but it was clear to Brody that holding Annabelle was the most practical thing to do to help Kate. And he was on Kate's team now. He wanted Kate to know they were a team.

"You do know what's bothering her, right?" There was amusement in Kate's tone, laced with an obvious challenge.

"I can guess," said Brody.

"You're not scared?"

"I'm made of pretty stern stuff."

"Okay, tough guy. Change table's over there if you're up for it."

Rex laughed more clearly this time.

Brody had no intention of backing down. It would take more than a teeny, tiny little girl to do him in.

"I've got this," he told Kate and received a twinkling grin in return. He realized he'd change a dozen diapers in order to put that expression on her face.

Then she turned her attention to Rex. But at least

she wasn't smiling at him. Brody was grateful for that. And a little smug, too.

"We're working with nine-foot ceilings," she said.

Brody muttered softly to Annabelle. "I'd say we're working with a twenty-six-inch baby."

"I heard that," said Kate, laughter in her voice.

"Your auntie is a meddler," he said to Annabelle, moving to the change table.

He knew they'd need a new diaper. He understood the concept of wet wipes. On the shelf below the table was an assortment of items, including a jar of diaper cream. And there was a covered trash can beside the table. He was sure he could work this all out.

He laid Annabelle down on the vinyl changing pad.

"Careful she doesn't roll off," Kate called.

"Careful you make your lines straight," he called back. "Meddler," he whispered to Annabelle.

Surprisingly, the baby smiled up at him.

"That's the spirit," he told her. Then he located a row of snaps down the inside leg of her stretchy sleeper.

He unfastened the garment and peeled it out of the way. She kicked her legs as soon as they were free, and she did try to roll. But he placed his palm on her tummy and gently held her in place.

He released the tapes on the diaper, memorizing their position for use with the fresh one. The smell immediately became stronger. He swallowed against a gag reflex, but he refused to give in.

Rex wasn't so lucky. He made a choking sound in the back of his throat and bolted for the exit.

Brody smiled between shallow breaths. But he also discovered an error in judgment. He should have retrieved the wet wipes before releasing the fasteners on the diaper.

"Got a problem?" asked Kate.

"We're fine."

But then she was beside him, the blue box of wipes open in her hand, offering them to him.

"Thanks," he said, taking one, shaking it out, and using it to make a pass over Annabelle's bottom.

"I'm impressed," said Kate.

"That I can clean a baby or keep my breakfast down?" He glanced meaningfully at the doorway where Rex had disappeared.

"Both," she said.

"At least we know how to get rid of Rex now."

"I expect he'll be back."

Brody helped himself to another wipe. "Oh, he'll be back. Don't encourage him."

"Encouraging him is the very last thing on my mind."

"Good." Brody had suspected as much, but he was glad to hear her say it.

"Do you think he's involved?"

"I'm not sure. He probably knows something. But I don't get the sense he's the key to anything. Don't try to spy on him."

The last thing Brody wanted was Kate trying to get close to Rex.

"But if an opportunity presents itself…" she said.

"No." He realized his tone was sharper than he'd intended.

Annabelle's face screwed up.

"It's okay, little girl," Brody crooned.

"I'm not saying I'll do anything risky," Kate said.

"Don't do anything at all. He's determined to make a move on you." And Brody was equally determined to keep that from happening.

"If he does, I might be able to use that."

"You're not your sister."

"Excuse me?" There was a challenge in her tone.

"I mean that in a good way."

"Are you saying I'm naive and unsophisticated?"

"I'm saying you're honest and…" He hesitated. "Okay, yeah, I'm saying you're maybe a little more innocent than Francie."

"I can take care of myself." She snapped the lid on the wipes container and put it back on the shelf. "I was doing great the past few days."

He dropped the soiled diaper into the trash. "But I'm here to help now, and we're a team."

"And you're the captain?"

"I'm…" He wasn't sure how to frame it. "I'm less vulnerable than you. I can't stay here twenty-four hours a day. So you'll be alone and unprotected."

"Quentin's here. And I don't get the sense that Rex will try anything in front of Quentin. All I'm going to do is keep my ear to the ground."

Rex took a diaper from the small pile. "I don't trust Quentin to protect you. Keep your ear to the ground, by all means. But make sure that ground is nowhere near Rex."

"Yes, sir. Would a snappy salute be in order?"

"Don't be melodramatic." He spread the clean diaper out beneath Annabelle.

"You've got it backwards," said Kate.

"How do I have it backwards?" Brody wanted to end this conversation. It was getting them nowhere. "I'm a man. If push comes to shove I have a good chance of taking Rex. Add to that, he doesn't have any sexual designs on me."

"I meant the diaper," she said. "You've got the diaper backwards."

He took in the orientation of the snowy white diaper. "Oh."

She reached out and turned it a hundred and eighty degrees. "There."

"Right. So, all that other stuff…"

"I get it. I'll be very careful. And I'll try to keep my distance from Rex."

"Try hard."

"Yes, sir." She gave him a mocking salute.

He shook his head as he folded the diaper around Annabelle and fastened the tapes. Then as he put her little feet back into the sleeper, he realized an oversight. "I forgot the cream."

Kate lifted Annabelle into her arms. "Don't worry. We'll get it next time."

His worry magnified as he gazed at Kate's small frame, her fresh face, the cherubic Annabelle cuddled in her arms. His thoughts went to his mother again, and how incredibly delighted she would be to have a daughter-in-law and a grandchild that looked just like that. He paused and couldn't help but smile—perhaps not so much the purple hair.

Kate gave Annabelle a kiss on the top of her head. "I just want this to be over."

"So do I."

He fought an urge to draw them both into his arms. He needed all this to be over so that his family would be financially secure. But he also wanted it to be over for Kate's sake, as well.

He stopped abruptly on that thought. When this was over, the two of them would be on opposite sides of the world. He was finding it hard to get excited by that prospect.

Ten

The soundproofing wallpaper, along with some quilted wall hangings, a couple of enormous stuffed animals and a white-noise machine seemed to do the trick for Annabelle. Kate had also discovered the room was equipped with a high-end baby monitor that came with an earpiece. So, once Annabelle was in bed that night, she was free to join everyone downstairs.

She'd looked through Francie's closet for something appropriate and had chosen a pair of purposely tattered denim shorts and a white lace top. Her midriff was bare. She'd spiked her short hair with gel. And her feet were clad in high-heeled white, chunky sandals.

She was ready to blend in and more than ready to hunt down Bert and Ernie.

"Hello, gorgeous," said Rex as he approached her.

He handed her a glass of champagne, the drink she'd decided early on to identify as her favorite. She'd chosen it because it was weaker than a martini, and because it had the air of extravagance. Also, she didn't mind the taste.

"Hi, Rex." She mustered up a smile.

He edged up close and wrapped an arm around her waist. "You look like someone ready to have fun."

"That's me," she singsonged. She desperately wanted to pull away, but she forced herself to endure the embrace.

"That's what I like about you," Rex whispered against her neck.

She caught Brody's glare. She assumed he was angry with her for not staying away from Rex. But the glare was aimed squarely at Rex, and it was intent. For a horrible second she thought Brody was going to stomp over and tear Rex limb from limb.

She quickly put some space between herself and Rex, pasting a carefree expression on her face. "I'm going to look for Quentin. We can catch up later?"

Rex reached out and grasped her hand. "Not so fast."

She forced herself to giggle in an effort to defuse

the situation. "In these shoes? I guarantee you, I'll be going really, really slow."

Rex glanced down at her shoes, and she took the opportunity to pull away. She kept her momentum going, sauntering toward the pool, making sure she mixed with the crowd.

Brody came up beside her. "What happened to the plan to stay away from him?"

"He approached me."

"No kidding." He glanced at her outfit. "And there's a lineup forming after him."

"I'm wearing Francie's clothes. I can't change back to me."

"That was the best she had?"

"It was one of the things she had. There were worse things in that closet."

"You're all but wearing a neon sign that says 'make a pass at me, because I'll probably say yes.'"

"Now who's being melodramatic?"

"You can't be that oblivious to how men react to you."

"And you can't be that paranoid. This party's full of people. I look flirty. I'm trying to look flirty. It's part of the plan."

She'd been wearing funky clothes for days now— she couldn't understand why Brody was suddenly so worried about it.

"Look further into her closet. There has to be something better than this."

"Focus, Brody. Have you seen Bert and Ernie?"

Brody let out an exaggerated sigh. "They're beside the gazebo, checking out the woman in the pink net cover-up."

Kate casually glanced in their direction. "And you say *I'm* dressed provocatively."

"She's trying harder, but it takes you less effort to have the same effect."

"Is that a compliment?" She truly wasn't sure.

"It's a compliment. And it's a warning. You have a lot of power. Use it wisely."

She coughed out a laugh. "You're losing it, Brody."

The bar was next to Bert and Ernie, so she quickly downed her champagne and handed the glass to Brody.

"You sure that was a good idea?"

"I'm going to the bar for a fresh drink."

"You could have dumped it in a plant."

"Didn't think of that." She had to admit, it would probably have been a better idea.

Just then, the wind shifted. She caught a whiff of smoke and wondered if they were doing burgers and brats again tonight. It reminded her that she was hungry. She hadn't wanted to eat much before prancing around in such a revealing outfit, but maybe she could snag one a little later on. In fact, she'd have two because—

Someone screamed.

"Not again," Kate muttered. She truly wished they'd stop tossing people into the pool.

But then someone shouted the word "fire!"

Her heart all but stopped.

Before she could turn to look, Brody was running. While others fled the flames that were curling up the side of the house to the second floor, he was running toward them.

Annabelle. Fear overtook Kate.

She started to run, almost instantly tripping up due to the shoes and falling to the grass. She kicked them off and jumped to her feet, running barefoot into the house.

She sprinted through the kitchen, down the hall and up the stairs. The smoke was coming in through the open windows, stinging her eyes. Though she was moving as fast as she could, she felt like she was running through wet concrete.

She finally made it to the nursery and wrenched open the door. Annabelle was still asleep. Faint bands of smoke hovered in the light from the window. She looked to be perfectly fine.

Kate scooped her up in her blanket, covering her head and face, then rushed out the door. The return trip seemed to go faster. And by the time she was outside, the flames were out.

Brody was standing over a charred lounger with a fire extinguisher in his hand. A burned wicker basket stood nearby. The wall was scorched at least twelve feet in the air.

Quentin clapped Brody on the back. "That was awesome." His voice was slurred, and he stumbled a little, steadying himself on Brody's shoulder.

Somebody let out a whoop.

"It's all clear, folks," Quentin yelled, turning to the crowd.

The music started up again, and everybody cheered.

Kate stared at Brody's rigid posture as Annabelle squirmed in her arms. She told herself, if she hadn't been there, Quentin would have remembered he had a baby. If the fire had gotten worse, surely he would have rescued Annabelle.

But then a shudder went through Kate's body, because she wasn't certain at all.

Even with the distraction of the fire, it was 3:00 a.m. before the party broke up. Brody was appalled by the behavior of the party guests. Even Quentin seemed to think it was funny that his house had nearly burned down.

Speculation was that someone had disposed of a cigarette butt in a towel hamper. The hamper had ignited, the fire spreading to the teak lounger beside it and up the wall of the house.

Once it was out, Kate had taken Annabelle back to the nursery. She hadn't returned to the party. Brody didn't blame her. Bert and Ernie would have to wait until tomorrow.

Brody was horrified to think about how badly it could have gone. He was sick of hanging out with Quentin and his friends. He didn't want Kate near any of them, and Annabelle seemed to be in genuine danger.

He needed to get the evidence he required and turn this whole thing over to the police. It was late, and the mansion was finally quiet, though adrenaline was still pumping through his system.

He marched into Quentin's office and sat down at his computer. He turned it on and dialed Will.

"Hello?" Will's voice was groggy.

"I'm at his computer," Brody said without preamble. "Tell me what I'm looking for."

Will became alert. "You're looking for a network connection."

Brody went to the control panel. "I see three."

"Read them to me."

Raised voices sounded down the hallway.

"Hang on," said Brody.

"What?"

Brody came to his feet, moving toward the door.

"We've already had this conversation," Quentin shouted.

"Gotta go," Brody said to Will, ending the call.

Brody pocketed his phone and carefully cracked the office door, peering out. The hallway was dim, but he could make out three figures.

"I'm going to bed," Quentin stated with determination.

He marched up the staircase and disappeared.

Bert said something to Ernie, and then Ernie answered back. The exchange became heated, and they moved down the hall, entering another room and shutting the door.

Brody knew he needed Kate right now. He hated to drag her out of bed after the evening she'd had, but he needed to know what those two were saying.

He left the office and took the stairs two at a time, letting himself into her bedroom. In the dim light, he quietly closed the connecting door to the nursery.

"Kate?" he whispered. He flicked on the bedside lamp.

"Kate?" he repeated. "It's Brody."

She blinked her eyes. For some reason, she didn't seem surprised to see him. "What's going on?"

"Can you come downstairs?"

She glanced at the clock on her bedside table. "It's after four."

"Bert and Ernie are having a fight. I need to know what they're arguing about."

She gave herself a little shake. "Sure. Yeah. Okay."

"You awake?" he asked.

She nodded. She flipped back the covers and rose from the bed. She was dressed in a pair of shorts and an old T-shirt. The outfit suited her, and her tousled hair and sleepy eyes were incredibly sexy.

He told himself to get a grip. "They're downstairs."

"Okay." She padded silently beside him.

"If they come out," Brody whispered to her as they descended the stairs. "If anyone sees us."

"You can pretend it's a tryst."

"I think that's best."

"They'll buy it. I have it on good authority that I looked provocative earlier tonight."

He couldn't believe she was making jokes. "We should be quiet."

She stopped talking.

They came to the closed door at the end of the hallway. The men's voices were muffled but audible.

"Something about a Mr. Kozak," she whispered.

It was the same name that came up before. Will

had looked into the name but found far too many Kozaks to know who they might be talking about.

"Whoever he is," Kate said. "He's coming to California tomorrow, and they need to pick him up at the airport."

She listened a few minutes longer. "They're back to Ceci again. If Quentin doesn't agree to Ceci, they're going to…" Kate went pale.

"What is it?" Brody asked.

Kate's voice dropped to a whisper. "They're going to threaten Annabelle. They want to use her to control Quentin."

Kate swayed, and Brody grasped her shoulders to support her.

"Brody, what do we do?"

He'd heard enough. "Let's go."

She stumbled as she followed him. "What are we going to do?"

Turning into Quentin's office, he pressed his speed dial for Will. "Whatever it is we need to find, we're doing it now."

He closed the door, locking them inside the office. He sat down behind the computer.

"They're threatening Annabelle," he told Will. "And we're running out of time."

Will's tone turned all business. "You're at the computer?"

"Yes."

"Read me the name of each of the network connections."

Brody read, and Will asked more questions, becoming more technical the deeper they went.

Kate paced the floor.

"Okay," Will finally said. "That's it. That's the proof."

Brody could hardly believe it. "We found it?"

Kate looked sharply up.

"It's time to call the police. I know exactly where to point them."

"Good. That's good." Brody was afraid to hope it would all come together. "Tell them the guy named Kozak is coming into the country tomorrow. Whoever he is, he's got to be connected somehow. Can you take another look for him?"

"Will do," said Will.

"And something about someone named Ceci. They keep saying they want Quentin to do something with Ceci. He's resisting, and that's why they're threatening Annabelle."

Will was silent.

"You there?" Brody asked.

"You know for sure that Ceci's a person?" asked Will.

Brody looked to Kate. "Ceci's a person?"

"I believe so. It's the only thing that makes sense."

"That's Kate's best guess."

"Did they ever actually say it wasn't something else?" Will asked.

Brody relayed the question.

She shook her head. "Not explicitly."

Brody went back to Will. "We thought maybe Kozak wanted Quentin to date or marry someone named Ceci. Maybe he has another illegitimate child out there?"

Will took another pause before responding. "Why would Bert and Ernie care about Quentin's love life?"

"It was only a theory."

"Got any other theories?"

"None. Do you?"

"Tell me exactly what they said about Ceci."

"I'll give you Kate." Brody handed Kate the phone. "He wants to know exactly what they said about Ceci."

She took the phone. "Hi, Will. This is Kate." She paused, obviously listening. "At first I thought they said Quentin would have to embrace Ceci, but then I thought maybe it was more closely translated to accept Ceci."

She paused. "Is this important? Because I'm not very good at translation. I don't want to mislead you."

Kate paused again. "No, they didn't. Okay."

She handed the phone back to Brody.

"Did that help?" he asked Will.

"Oh, man," Will said.

"In a good way or a bad way?"

"Ceci."

"You do realize that wasn't an answer."

"It's not Ceci, it's C E S I." There was stark astonishment in Will's voice.

"That made even less sense." Brody wished he could reach through the phone line and shake Will's brain back to life.

"CESI isn't a woman, it's an acronym. It stands for Cryptography Enabled Steganography Instances."

"Was that English?"

"Steganography hides messages inside other objects. Cryptography encrypts those messages."

"What kind of messages?"

"Any kind of message." Will's level of excitement was clearly growing. "Any kind of data."

A lightbulb went off inside Brody's brain. "Kozak wants to use 'Blue Strata Combat' to move secret data, hidden data."

"That would be my guess," Will said.

"To millions of computers worldwide?"

"Yes. Do you have any idea what this could be?"

An unnerving picture was forming in Brody's

mind. "Through millions of servers, into countless countries."

"This is way above my pay grade."

"Could it be financial data?" Brody's astonishment and worry were both growing as the moments passed. This had to go far beyond stealing computer gaming code.

"It could be financial," said Will. "Or something even more sinister. It could be trade secrets, or even military secrets."

"Are we talking national security?" Brody asked.

"You need to get back here," Will said. "We have to call FBI Cyber Crimes."

"I'm not leaving Kate."

Brody's words caught her attention. Worry was etched in her face.

"You should get Kate and Annabelle out of the house as soon as you can."

"Agreed," Brody said. He wasn't leaving them in danger any longer.

Kate tried to quell her nerves as she packed a diaper bag for Annabelle. It was barely five in the morning, so they'd be gone long before Quentin woke up. But she couldn't quell her nervousness.

She wasn't taking much. If they got caught leaving, she wanted her story of taking Annabelle for a drive to put her back to sleep to sound plausible. And she could buy anything they needed in the short term.

As soon as Quentin was arrested, she'd try for temporary custody of Annabelle. Once she had that, she was taking the baby to Seattle. Annabelle would be safe there. She'd be safe and she would be happy.

Kate zipped up the bag, afraid to believe it might be almost over.

She slung it over her shoulder and took Annabelle in her arms, stopping at the kitchen for a bottle. Brody was moving the car seat to his car and would meet them out front.

Annabelle whimpered as they made their way down the stairs.

"Shhh," Kate whispered. "We'll get you a bottle, honey. It's coming right up."

Kate removed a bottle from the fridge and warmed it in the microwave. While she waited, every sound seemed magnified. She imagined she could hear Brody's car out front, and Annabelle's soft cries seemed to echo in the room. The microwave's beeps sounded piercing sharp.

"You're not nearly so sexy with a baby weighing you down."

Kate cringed at the tone of Rex's voice.

"I'm not trying to look sexy," she said, trying to sound casual.

"Going somewhere?"

"For a drive. Annabelle's fussy, and it quiets her down."

Rex moved closer. "Doesn't a bottle usually work?"

"Sometimes. But a drive works better."

Kate tested the formula temperature on her wrist. Thankfully, it was just right. While she'd prayed Annabelle would stay quiet, she now wished the baby would make some noise. It would add credibility to her story about going for a drive.

"Thing is," Rex said. "You don't have a car."

His words flustered her, and she hesitated. It was just for a moment, but she could tell it was enough to raise his suspicions.

"Brody offered to drive," she said, collecting the baby, her supplies and moving for the door.

"What's Brody doing here?"

"I... I..."

Rex's eyes narrowed.

"I slept with him," she blurted out. "I slept with Brody. That's why he's here in the morning."

"Why don't I believe you?"

She tried a pout. "Why would I lie about that?"

Rex gave his head a slow shake. "I don't know."

She tried to intimidate him. "Who I sleep with is no concern of yours."

"Maybe not," he said, stepping fully into the center of the door, blocking her path. "But what goes on in this house is my business."

"Sex doesn't normally go on in this house?" She tried to be sarcastic.

"People don't normally leave with Quentin's daughter."

Kate's stomach lurched. What did Rex know? What did he suspect?

"I say we go talk to Quentin," he said.

"Quentin's asleep." She could feel her courage deserting her. Her heart rate was spiking and her mouth had turned dry.

"We'll wake him up," suggested Rex.

"We shouldn't do that."

"Oh, I think we should." Rex's hand clamped onto her arm.

There was no way to fight him off, not with her holding Annabelle. She scrambled for the right action. Should she try to make a run for it, should she yell, or should she brazen it out and hope Quentin fell for the story?

He normally didn't care what went on with Annabelle as long as it didn't cause him any trouble. If she held off on the bottle a few more minutes, Annabelle would start crying. Quentin hated it when Annabelle cried. He'd agree to anything so long as Kate was taking her out of earshot.

"Fine," she said, giving him a defiant look. "Let's wake Quentin up. But you better be ready to tell him it was your great idea."

Rex tugged on her arm, urging her down the hall.

"You can let me go," she said.

"I don't think so."

He marched her up the stairs and down the hall to the master bedroom.

He banged on the door. "Quentin?"

Annabelle started to cry.

"Shhh," Kate said automatically. But she was secretly cheering for the baby's lungs.

The door flung open, and Quentin appeared. "What the hell is going on out here?"

"Kate is taking Annabelle," Rex said.

"For a drive," Kate quickly put in.

"With Brody." Rex frowned.

"What the hell time is it?" Quentin bellowed.

Annabelle cried louder.

There was a sudden commotion on the first floor. There were loud shouts and running feet. It took Kate a second for the words to make sense.

"FBI! FBI! Everybody out where we can see you!"

Before she could react, Rex shoved her through the bedroom door and locked it behind them.

"What are you doing?" she demanded. She looked

to Quentin, hoping against hope he would intervene. Surely he cared about the safety of his own daughter.

Then Rex pulled a gun from beneath his shirt and trained it on her. She automatically turned to protect Annabelle.

"What on earth is going on?" Her voice quavered with fear.

"You tell me," Quentin shouted.

"I don't know." Kate was becoming terrified.

Where was Brody? Was he going to be able to help her?

"Start talking," Rex growled.

"I don't know what's going on," Kate cried. "Put down the gun. You might hurt Annabelle."

"Annabelle is the least of your worries," Rex said.

Kate held the baby closer to her chest.

Annabelle kept crying.

"She knows," Rex said to Quentin.

"I don't know anything," Kate said.

Somebody banged loudly on the bedroom door. "FBI. Everybody out. Hands in the air."

"We have a baby in here," Rex shouted back.

The door burst open, and two armed men entered the room.

Rex grabbed Kate and pushed the gun to her chest.

"Let Annabelle go," Kate pleaded. "Just let me put her down on the bed."

"No," Rex growled.

"Quentin," Kate pleaded. "She's your daughter. Please don't let her get hurt."

Quentin looked like he was making up his mind.

"Quentin!" She couldn't believe he was hesitating.

"Quiet, ma'am," one of the officers ordered sharply.

Kate's panic was rising. She couldn't think straight. She didn't know what to do. She couldn't just stand here with Annabelle's life in danger.

"Take me," she told Rex. "You don't need Annabelle."

"Shut her up," Quentin demanded.

"I can give her the bottle," Kate said. "Let me put her on the bed. She can have the bottle. Then she'll keep quiet."

"Quiet, ma'am," the officer ordered again.

Kate wasn't inclined to listen to him. He wasn't likely to shoot her. Rex just might.

"We're walking out of here," Rex spat.

"We can't let you do that," the officer said.

"You can't stop me. Come on, Quentin."

"We have a search warrant for the premises," the officer said. "Are you Quentin Roo?"

"And we have hostages." Rex sneered at the man.

"Let them go," the other officer said.

Kate knew she was probably losing it, but she couldn't help but think it was about time they made that suggestion. Shouldn't that have been the first thing they said? Please let go of the nice hostages?

Rex started to push her toward the door.

"No closer," the officer ordered.

Rex ignored him.

Quentin moved in. He reached for Annabelle.

"No," Kate moaned, clasping the baby tighter.

"Give her to me," Quentin said.

"No. You can't."

"She's my daughter." He pulled hard, and Kate was terrified.

A split second later, Annabelle was in Quentin's arms. Rex had Kate held tight, and they were moving toward the door.

She stared at the officers. Surely, they wouldn't let them past. They'd do something, disarm Rex or shoot him or something.

"Out of the way," Rex shouted. "Get back!"

Annabelle's cries reached a new decibel.

"Shut up," Quentin muttered to the baby.

When the FBI agents stepped aside, Kate's terror rose to a whole new level.

Rex forced her down the stairs. The four made their way through the entry hall and out the front door.

There, they were surrounded by a dozen armed officers.

"Give yourselves up," someone shouted over a megaphone. "There's nowhere to go."

"What do we do?" Quentin asked Rex.

"Let us go," Kate said.

"Shut up," Rex demanded. "We'll take your car," he said to Quentin.

"There's no way out," the megaphone man said.

"They've blocked the driveway," Quentin said.

"We've got hostages," Rex called out and kept walking.

Suddenly, Brody was standing in front of them. "Release them."

"I should have known," Rex said. "There was always something off about you. Didn't I tell you that?" he asked Quentin. "FBI?" he asked Brody.

"No," Brody said. "But give me Annabelle and let Kate go."

"Not a chance."

"The only way out of here is through me."

"My pleasure."

"That's murder," Brody said calmly. "You want to be arrested for corporate espionage or murder. You want a white-collar prison or the death penalty?" He looked to Quentin. "You'll be charged, too."

"Big talk," Rex sputtered.

Brody didn't move a muscle. "I'm not bluffing. Let her go, or shoot me. It's one or the other."

Rex aimed his gun at Brody.

"Brody, no." Kate was overcome with sheer, blind panic.

She saw Rex's face, and she knew in her soul that he was going to shoot Brody. Brody was going to die right here on the front steps.

Before she could even think about it, she was pushing Rex with all her might. A shot rang out. Brody lunged forward. He grabbed Annabelle from Quentin's arms.

"Down," he screamed at Kate.

The world went into slow motion. She looked straight in his eyes, and did exactly as he asked. She dropped down, lying flat on her stomach while Brody covered Annabelle with his body.

More shots echoed.

She covered her ears, and squeezed her eyes shut.

"Kate." It was Brody's voice. His hand touched hers. "Kate."

She blinked to find him lying beside her, Annabelle still crying in his arms.

"I have her bottle," she said.

"Are you all right?" he asked.

She nodded. She was sore, but she didn't think she was injured. "Is it over?"

"It's over."

"Are they…" She swallowed, looking around at the chaos. She couldn't finish the sentence.

"Don't worry about it right now. Don't look back. Don't look at anything." He led her up the front steps. "Just focus on the house, Kate. And hand me the bottle."

Eleven

The hotel had brought a crib up to Brody's suite, and Annabelle was now sound asleep. It had been a long day. He and Kate had given statements to the FBI, who had picked Kozak up at the airport. There they'd also arrested Bert and Ernie who'd come to meet him.

Will was now working with the FBI IT experts, determining the extent of the theft from Shetland Technologies and whether or not they'd managed to use the cryptography enabled steganography to commit any other crimes.

Brody wanted nothing more than to be here with Kate and Annabelle. He carried two snifters of cognac to the sofa where she was curled up.

"Kate, you holding up okay?" he asked, handing one to her.

She didn't answer, and she didn't take the drink, so he set it down on the coffee table in front of her.

"It may take a while," he said, sitting down beside her.

She was silent for a moment more. "I can't believe it's over."

"It's over."

"He was going to shoot you."

"I don't think so."

Her voice rose. "Did you see his expression, his eyes? I saw it in his eyes, Brody. Rex was going to shoot you point-blank."

Brody leaned across her knee to pick up the glass. This time when he handed it to her, she took it.

"It's over," he repeated with finality, and he clinked his snifter to hers.

She stared into space.

"You should drink now," he told her.

She took a sip. "You just stood there, a great big target only five feet away. You wouldn't move."

"I wasn't about to let him take you and Annabelle."

"But he had a gun." She waved the glass. "The cops. They were smart. They let him by. But you... You..."

"The cops don't know you the way I do."

She gave him a quizzical look, but he wasn't ready to elaborate on that statement.

He swallowed some of his cognac. It tasted good going down. "You were smart to push him off balance."

"I had to do something. He was going to kill you, Brody. I'm positive of that, and there's nothing you can say to change my mind."

"Okay. He was going to kill me."

For some reason, that seemed to satisfy her. She turned on the sofa, coming up on her knees. "You saved my life. You saved Annabelle's life."

"Listen, we can talk about this as long as you like, or as long as you need to in order to feel better. But I did what I had to do, and so did you, and everybody is okay. Well, everybody that counts, anyway."

She paused. But then her shoulders dropped, and the intensity went out of her expression.

"We can stop talking about it now," she said.

He was dying to touch her, so he smoothed back her hair. "We've got the emergency custody hearing tomorrow afternoon."

She trapped his hand and kissed his palm. "Thanks to you."

He set down his glass. "It was nothing. You deserve Annabelle, and Annabelle deserves you. Quentin is gone from her life."

Kate's hand started to shake, and Brody took her glass, setting it next to his on the table.

"I can't believe he's dead," she said in a quiet voice.

"It's sad. It didn't have to happen like that."

She nodded. "I hope Annabelle won't have any memories of what had happened."

"She won't. She's so young."

"I shouldn't repeat it now that Rex is dead, but I really didn't like that man."

Brody leaned in, pulled her forward and kissed the top of her head. "You must be tired."

"I'm numb."

"Let's go to bed." He realized he was sounding and acting presumptuous. "I mean, I can convert the sofa and sleep out here, if you'd rather."

She tipped her head to look up at him, giving a ghost of a smile. "We can share the bed. I'd like to share the bed."

"Good." He wasn't near ready to let her go.

He rose and held out his hand to her, walking her into the bedroom where he pulled back the quilt. They both took off their clothes and climbed in.

He drew her into his arms, and she was asleep in moments.

He gazed at her pink cheeks, her cute little nose and the dark eyelashes resting against her skin. He touched her crazy purple hair and smiled. She'd done that for Annabelle, for a niece she'd never even met. She'd chopped off her hair and walked boldly into Quentin Roo's stronghold and took him on.

With all the dysfunctionality in her upbringing, with her estrangement from her sister, she'd still stepped up.

He couldn't help comparing Kate's family to his own. The Calders weren't as close as some, and they'd had their share of scandal and betrayal in past generations, but he liked to think he'd do anything for his brother, Blane.

The family was small right now. His father had only one sibling. A sister, and she'd died in a horse-back riding accident in her twenties. She hadn't married and had no children.

Brody's father was late to marry, and his grandparents had passed away a few years back. Brody and his brother, Blane, were now the future of the Calder dynasty. They were expected to marry and produce heirs, and that was fine with Brody.

He'd always looked forward to children. He'd decided a long time ago to have as many as he could. But having children meant finding a woman willing to take him on.

Up to now, he hadn't found the time to focus on that facet of his life. He'd dated, and there was no shortage of women with a romantic notion of what it meant to marry into the Calder family. Some of them seemed like wonderful people. But it wasn't just a matter of compatibility. It was no small thing for anyone to take on the demands of joining the nobility.

As the second son, his social obligations were far less intense than his brother's. But given Blane's health problems, Brody expected to spend a considerable amount of time supporting Blane. His future wife would have to be prepared for the reality of that life.

Aside from the complications of his family, the past few years had been focused on business. If he couldn't save the family fortune, there'd be nothing to pass on to any children of his or of Blane's.

He realized he ought to share the good news. He calculated the time zone difference, and guessed Blane would be up and around.

He dialed the number and let it ring.

He was about to give up when the line connected.

"Brody?" To his surprise, it was his mother's crisp voice.

"Hello, Mother." He kept his voice low so he wouldn't disturb Kate. He couldn't help but feel disappointed. He'd wanted Blane to be the first to hear the news.

"Blane can't talk right now, Brody." She seemed annoyed about something.

"Are you sure?" Brody was certain Blane would want to interrupt anything he might be doing for this. But he didn't want to tell his mother it was important, because she'd ask to hear the news herself.

"Give me the phone." Blane's voice was faint in the background.

"Is he with you?" Brody was surprised his mother would scoop Blane's phone right from under his nose. That was high-handed even for her.

"He can't talk," his mother said in her most officious countess voice.

"Why not?"

"He's with the doctor."

Brody went on alert, sitting up straight, remembering his last conversation with Blane. "What doctor? Where are you?"

"We're at the hospital."

"Is it the cough?"

Kate blinked her eyes open.

"Sorry," he mouthed to her, regretting waking her.

"It's his lungs," said his mother. "They're doing tests."

There was coughing in the background.

"What kind of tests?" asked Brody, his attention turning fully to the phone call.

"We'll know more when they're done. It might be congestion, or there might be deterioration."

"Deterioration of his lungs?" Brody's worry was now in full force.

"Give me the—" Blane's voice turned to coughing again.

Brody met Kate's eyes.

"I'll call you back," his mother said.

"But—"

"They say we'll know more later tonight," she said. "Call me as soon as you know anything at all."

"I will. But since you're not here…"

Guilt spiked in Brody. "What I'm doing here is important, Mother."

"Maybe so."

Blane spoke in the background again. "Mother, don't."

"As you say," she said to Brody.

"Call me," he reminded her.

"Fine."

The conversation ended.

Kate moved into a sitting position "Who was that?"

"My mother."

"Something's wrong." It wasn't a question.

"My brother, Blane," said Brody, staring at his phone.

"Is he ill?"

"Yes. He has a condition called Newis Bar Syndrome. It's a rare neuromuscular disease."

She dipped her head to his shoulder and gave him a gentle kiss. "I'm so sorry to hear that."

"He may have developed a complication."

"Oh, Brody."

"Deterioration of his lungs." Brody could barely say it out loud. It sounded very serious, even critical.

His brother couldn't be critically ill. Blane had an important future. He had to inherit the earldom. He had to get married, have children, produce the new viscount and other heirs.

Kate shifted next to Brody, wrapping her hand around his arm and leaning in close. "Is there anything I can do?"

"No. Not tonight. I know he's getting the very best care. I wanted to tell him about Shetland Tech." Brody had looked forward to telling Blane directly. "Maybe I should have told my mother. The good news might give him a lift."

Kate tucked her arms around his neck and just stayed there, silently holding him close. After her traumatic day, he found it nothing short of amazing that she had it in her to comfort him.

He hugged her back, burying his face against her fragrant hair and closing his mind to everything but the peace she seemed to bring to his world.

Her small body curled against him, soft and yielding. He held her close, feeling her heartbeat, his chest hollowing out with emotion. He touched her face. Then he gave in and kissed her neck.

She smoothed her palm over his cheek, then she cradled his face, drawing back, gazing deeply into his eyes. He willed her lips to his, and she moved toward him, her kiss a gentle whisper of empathy.

He kissed her back, then again, and again. Desire flowed through him like honey.

"Is this okay?" he whispered.

"Yes," she returned, her kisses growing deeper. "It's…" She arched against him. "Good."

He splayed a hand across her back, turning her into the soft bed. Her crazy hair stood out against the white pillow, her breasts rose and fell with her breaths, her pink nipples beautiful in the dim light. He loved her breasts. They were soft, smooth coral-tipped wonders. He loved her neck, her stomach, her face. He could have gazed at her for eternity.

Desire, tenderness and hope all rose within him, neutralizing the exhaustion of the day.

He kissed her, then he kissed her again, then he deepened the kiss and let her essence fill him.

"You aren't too tired, are you?" He didn't want to be selfish. She'd been through enough.

"Don't stop," she whispered.

He moved on top of her, skin to skin. He ran his

hand from her shoulders down her back, to her hips and bottom, pulling her intimately against him.

"Oh, Brody."

"You bring out the best in me, Kate." His kisses roamed her neck and her bare shoulder, moving to the softness of her breasts.

"I need you," he rasped.

"You've got me. Please make love to me."

He'd never heard sweeter words. He eased her thighs apart, pressing slowly inside, drinking in every inch, every second as her heat surrounded him. And then he was inside her, rocking against her, kissing her tenderly, and feeling her heartbeat sync with his.

He closed his eyes and gave himself over to sensation. He could hear her breaths and her small moans. He could smell her scents, fresh and floral, deep and earthy. She was soft to his hard, gentle to his harsh.

He rode the sweet rhythm, until the waves grew larger, their crests going higher. He tried to hang on, never wanting the feeling to end.

But sweat broke out on his body. His muscle fibers tightened their way to the breaking point. He couldn't slow down. He had to speed up.

"Yes," she cried against his mouth. "Just...like..." Her body contracted around him, and he roared his way to paradise.

* * *

It was early.

Kate was sated and content in Brody's arms. The sun was barely filtering through the sheers on the hotel window. They had minutes, maybe seconds until Annabelle woke up.

Annabelle was an early riser, but a happy one.

"Did you know this could happen to your brother?" she asked Brody.

His brother's health scare was their one immediate worry.

"I didn't expect it." Brody was behind her, his body spooning hers, his arms wrapped around her. "There are dozens of potential complications. This is the first time it's hit his lungs."

"It must have been hard." She toyed with his fingers where they lay against her stomach. "To leave when Blane was sick."

"It was. But I had no choice. And he was doing quite well last time I saw him." Brody paused. "But I was the one who put my family's fortune at risk. And it was up to me to fix it."

"How did you do it? How did you put it at risk?"

"You going to make me show you my weakness, aren't you?"

"I'm going to make you be honest."

"And if I'd rather not tell you? If I'd rather you

thought of me as the brave and dashing hero who saved your life yesterday?"

"You're going to use that one for a long time to come, aren't you?"

He turned silent, and she regretted her words. They were too lighthearted for this conversation. And they were presumptuous. She was implying they'd be together for a while. He'd never suggested any such thing.

"I got into trouble because I got cocky," he said. "Blane and my father wanted to go into the hotel business. It's much safer, but the financial returns are low and a lot slower coming. We needed money right away, so I took a risk."

"And you lost the money?"

"Not at first. At first, I had some real success with software development. But I got carried away. I wanted to be the savior. I wanted Blane to be able to build his dream hotel and run it for years to come. I thought…"

Kate waited. "Thought what?"

"I thought if he could live his dream, his health might improve. I thought taking money worries off the table would allow him to get out and meet a great woman. But it had the opposite effect. When I lost the money, he worried even more."

"Did he meet a woman?" Kate hoped he had. If he was anything like Brody, he deserved to be happy.

"No. And now it may be too late."

She turned in Brody's arms. "Don't talk like that. They haven't found anything wrong with him yet."

"Except for Newis Bar Syndrome."

"Which he's had all along, and has nothing to do with anything you did or didn't do."

"It could be bad," he said.

She looked into his eyes. "And it could be nothing." She leaned across his chest and reached for his phone. "Call him again."

He accepted the phone but stared at it without dialing.

"Not knowing won't change anything," she said.

After a long moment, he pressed a number. Then he raised it to his ear.

It occurred to her that he might want privacy, so Kate started to rise. But he held her back.

"Stay right there," he said.

"Are you sure?"

"Yes." He slipped an arm around her shoulders and drew her close.

She settled in against him, trying not to feel too desperate about this stolen time together. Annabelle would wake soon, and they'd attend the custody hearing later today. Then Brody would return to Scotland.

And Kate would go back to Seattle. In the blink of an eye, this unexpected feeling of closeness would be nothing but a memory.

"Hey, Blane," Brody said.

Kate closed her eyes in relief. Then she let the timbre of his voice vibrate against her skin. She loved his voice.

"You feeling any better?" Brody asked.

Kate listened to his heartbeat, felt his chest rise and fall, smelled the tang of his sweat, and tasted the salt of his skin.

"They did?" Brody asked. He sounded relieved. "That's fantastic news. But don't go home too soon."

She couldn't help but smile.

Brody laughed. "You'll be dancing again in no time. But don't let Mother pick your suit." He paused. "I don't care if it's tradition. There'll be women there, eligible women. You need to look like you live in this century, not the last."

Brody absently stroked Kate's hair.

"You're a viscount, heir to an earldom. You're eligible already." He chuckled again. "You use what you've got, man."

Kate felt a sudden desire to meet Blane. It was clear the two brothers had a close relationship. Was he as smart and interesting as Brody? It was hard to imagine there were two such men in the world.

Then just as quickly as the idea had formed, it disappeared. She knew it would never happen.

"I have more good news," Brody said, pure joy evident in his tone. "Our cash flow problem is solved. It's a bit of a long story, one you don't have to worry about right now. But nobody will be illegally using our intellectual property."

Kate gave him a hug, remembering yesterday all over again, gratitude blooming inside her.

"I can, and I will," he said. "Soon. You rest and get better."

Brody signed off and set down his phone.

"That sounded good," she said.

"It was only congestion. His lungs are fine, and he's on the road to recovery."

"I'm so glad to hear that."

Brody slid down in the bed and cuddled her closer. "It's a huge relief."

They both lay quiet for a few minutes.

"They didn't know the details, did they?" she asked him. "Your family didn't know what you were doing over here."

If they'd known about Quentin, Brody's brother would surely have asked some far more specific questions.

"I didn't want to worry them all. There was nothing they could do, and I was hoping I could solve it before we went bankrupt."

"Bankrupt?"

"It was a possibility. If Beast Blue had made it to market first with their game, Shetland would have folded. And with the loan guarantees we signed, we'd have lost the castle."

She turned her head to look up at him. "I can't believe you have a castle."

"It's on the River Tay."

"It's a *castle*." Its location wasn't the most pertinent information as far as Kate was concerned. She was trying to come to grips with Brody's expansive lifestyle, his family, Brody himself.

"It's not as exciting as it sounds. It's old and pretty drafty. It's been in my family for twenty-two generations."

"I'm sorry, Brody. One more time. You have a castle?"

"We're the Scottish nobility, Kate. Everyone has a castle."

"I have a thousand-square-foot condo," she said, mustering up a faux note of superiority.

"You told me that." There was answering humor in his tone.

"It's been in my family for nearly a year."

"That's impressive."

"Well, half of it, anyway. My friend Nadia owns the other half."

"I bet it's not drafty."

"Tight as a drum."

"I'd like to see it sometime."

"Well, you coming to Seattle seems a lot more likely than me going to Scotland."

"I'm serious." He sat up. "It makes sense. I'll go with you and Annabelle to Seattle."

She couldn't tell if they were still joking. He seemed serious, but he wasn't making sense. "We don't need an escort. The danger is past."

As if hearing her name, Annabelle vocalized from her crib in the living room.

"I've become invested in the little tyke," he said. "I want to make sure she's in a good place. I'm definitely coming to the hearing."

"My condo is a good place. It might not be a castle, but it has everything she needs."

"I didn't mean it that way."

"What way did you mean it?"

"I want to make sure she stays with you."

Kate rose from the bed and retrieved one of the hotel robes, tightening it around her waist. "Is this because you changed her diaper?"

"I like to think we bonded over that."

She couldn't help injecting a note of teasing sarcasm. "You were definitely her knight in shining armor."

He got up and shrugged into the other robe. "A few generations ago. Yeah, I could have done that."

"Can you ride a horse?" she asked, moving into the living room to get Annabelle.

"I play polo," he called from behind her.

"Oooh, la di da. Hello, sweetheart," she crooned to a smiling Annabelle. "Uncle Brody is here to change your diaper."

"Walked right into that one, didn't I?"

"Yes, you did." Kate lifted Annabelle and handed her off to Brody.

Twelve

The more Brody thought about it, the better he liked the idea of going to Seattle. It would take Will a few more days to tie up loose ends in LA. They'd already put a team of lawyers on the case to make sure *i*'s were dotted and *t*'s crossed. It would take months for the techs to go through Beast Blue's code.

Brody could stay in LA until Will was done, or he could take a quick trip to Seattle, get Annabelle settled. Then he could come back to close things off before he returned to Scotland.

For today, he'd borrowed one of the lawyers at their newly engaged firm to help with Annabelle's case. Brody was encouraged by Kalvin Moran's youth. He knew the firm was anxious to please Shetland Tech, so if they'd put a junior associate onto Annabelle, that meant they expected it to be straightforward.

It was a small hearing room, with a single row of chairs behind the lawyer's tables.

"Ms. Dunhern is the child's aunt?" the judge asked Kalvin.

"Yes."

"Is she the only known relative?"

"Mr. Roo's parents are deceased. He has a half brother who is currently incarcerated in Illinois."

The judge read a paper on her desk. "The child's grandmother, Chloe Dunhern is—"

"Right here," came a smoke-husky voice from the back of the courtroom.

Brody turned along with everyone else to see a sixtysomething woman with spiky, dyed-blond hair walk shakily into the hearing room. She wore a pair of skintight black-and-white diamond-patterned slacks and a royal blue sleeveless sweater.

"Oh, no," Kate groaned beside him.

"I'm Annabelle's grandmother," she announced with a little wave.

"Mom, please," Kate said.

"Are you petitioning the court for custody?" the judge asked.

"Yes," Chloe Dunhern said. "Yes, that's right."

"You can't have custody, Mom."

"Hello, Kate. I don't see why not." Chloe pointed her finger. "You're just after the money."

"Please address me," the judge said.

"Yes, Your Honor," Chloe said. "Where do I sit?"

Kate leaned over to Kalvin. "Ask her if she's been drinking."

"She's not a witness," Kalvin said.

"Can you ask?"

Kalvin stood up. "Your Honor, can you ask Ms. Dunhern, Ms. Chloe Dunhern if she's been drinking?"

The judge's brows went up. "Ms. Dunhern, have you had anything to drink today?"

"Orange juice."

"Vodka," Kate whispered to Kalvin.

"Your honor, Ms. Dunhern has been known to drink vodka in her orange juice. Could we clarify if that's the case today?"

"Ms. Dunhern?" the judge asked.

"Yes?"

"Did you have vodka or any other alcohol in your orange juice."

"No."

"Breathalyzer," Kate whispered.

"Would Ms. Dunhern be willing to submit to a breathalyzer test?" Kalvin asked.

"Ms. Dunhern?" the judge asked.

"What about her?" Chloe asked, pointing at Kate while holding the back of a chair for support. "Nobody's asking Kate to take a breathalyzer."

Kalvin looked to Kate.

Kate nodded. "You bet."

"I'm ordering a breathalyzer test for both petitioners," the judge said.

"Well," Chloe said. "Well, in that case..." She seemed uncertain about what to do.

"Mom, we've talked about this," Kate said, sounding carefully patient.

"We didn't agree on anything," Chloe said.

"We did agree, Mom. You're busy. You're tired. Annabelle will be a lot of work."

"I..." Chloe didn't seem to have an answer for that.

"Can we talk later?" Kate asked.

Chloe looked around at the participants, seeming to be making up her mind. "I don't need a breathalyzer." She stated emphatically. Then she turned and walked from the room.

"That's my mother," Kate said helplessly.

There was a moment of dazed silence.

"Your Honor," Kalvin continued, regrouping. "Other than, uh, Chloe Dunhern, Kate Dunhern is the child's only known relative. She's a teacher in the Seattle public school system. She owns residential real estate in Seattle. We've submitted work and personal references, along with her credit report. She has no criminal record, and is willing and able to care for Annabelle on an immediate and emergency basis."

The judge looked at Kate. "Have you had anything to drink today?"

"No, Your Honor."

"What is your average weekly consumption of alcohol?"

"Two to three drinks."

"Ever in the morning?"

"Only on Christmas Day. A mimosa with brunch."

"Very well." The judge brought down her gavel. "I've reviewed all the submitted documentation, including the police reports, and grant temporary custody of Annabelle Dunhern to Kate Dunhern."

Brody gave Kate's hand a quick squeeze.

"Thank you," she said to Kalvin.

"Happy to help out."

Brody shook Kalvin's hand. "Thanks."

"My pleasure, sir." Kalvin shut his briefcase and took his leave.

Brody pulled Kate into a hug. "Well done."

"You mean my not drinking in the mornings?"

"That little fact didn't hurt your case."

"That was so embarrassing."

"It was interesting to meet your mother. Whatever else she did, she raised a wonderful daughter."

"That's a very nice thing to say."

"I mean it." Brody put a hand on the small of her back as they walked from the hearing room. "Now, what should we do first? Plane tickets, baby gear, lawyer's office?"

Kate had already said she didn't want to go back to the mansion to pick up any of Anabelle's things. She had Annabelle and the chickadee necklace, and that was all she wanted. She was after a fresh start, and Brody didn't blame her.

"You don't need to babysit me, Brody."

"That's not what I'm doing."

"You must have things to do."

"I have a lot of things to do. But what I want to do is help you. Let's start with a lawyer."

"We just finished with a lawyer."

"That was step one. Next you need to hire someone to represent Annabelle's interests."

"They told me she'd have a court-appointed advocate."

"You still need a lawyer. It's going to be a complicated estate."

"What about Kalvin?"

"He's a junior associate, and Beast Blue is worth millions."

Brody couldn't help but wonder if Annabelle might be better served by someone more experienced. But it wasn't his decision. Kate's comfort level was what counted.

"I liked him."

"He is backed by a solid firm. So he would have the more senior partners to support him."

"We could ask him if he's interested."

Brody couldn't imagine any circumstance under which Kalvin wouldn't be interested. "Okay. Let's see if we can catch him in the lobby."

Kate was relieved to finally be home.

Nadia greeted them at the door, oohing and aahing over Annabelle, giving Kate a warm hug, and politely greeting Brody who carried in armloads of baby paraphernalia.

"Will you come to Auntie Nadia?" she cooed to Annabelle.

Annabelle looked perplexed for a moment, but then smiled.

Kate handed her over.

"We're going to get along just fine," Nadia sing-songed as she wandered away. "Do you want to see the kitchen?"

"Anywhere in particular I should put all this?" Brody asked.

"In the living room, I guess." Kate's condo suddenly felt small. "The bedrooms are upstairs, and there's room in the basement for storage. But I can see this is going to take some organizing."

"You're here," he said. "That's what counts."

Kate blew out a big breath of relief. "I'm here. And Annabelle's here. And everything else will work itself out."

Nadia reappeared. "Are you staying in Seattle?" she asked Brody.

There was something funny in her tone, but Kate couldn't put her finger on it.

"For a few days," Brody said.

"Downtown?"

Brody hesitated.

Kate realized they hadn't talked about where he'd stay. They'd spent the last three nights in his hotel suite. They'd slept together there—partly because there'd only been one bed, but mostly because their physical attraction had shown no signs of fading.

She wondered if she should ask him to stay at the condo. Should they continue to sleep together?

"I was going to check for a hotel nearby," he put in smoothly. Unless a person had been looking for it, the pause in the conversation was barely noticeable.

"The Seabreeze is about ten minutes away," Nadia said.

"I'll check them out." He set the packages down on the sofa.

"Good idea."

His expression was puzzled for a few seconds while he looked at Nadia. But then it softened, and he turned his attention to Kate. "Do you want to shop later on? You'll need a crib right away."

"Yes," Kate said, enthusiastically. "Are you going to be around this afternoon?" she asked Nadia.

"I can be here for this one." She gave Annabelle some mini kisses on her fingers, and Annabelle laughed.

"If I get Annabelle down for her nap before we go, do you mind watching her?"

"Not at all."

"It'll be a big help to pick up a few things right away."

"In the meantime," Brody said. "I'll go check out the hotel."

"Are you sure?" Kate asked. She felt like she was rushing him out the door. "Are you hungry? I can make us something for lunch."

"Don't worry about me." He gave her a squeeze on the shoulder. "I'll call you in a while."

"Okay."

It felt strange to have him leave. They'd been together pretty much constantly since the FBI raid. She realized she was coming to depend on him.

When the door closed behind him, she felt strangely alone.

"Tell me everything." Nadia pushed aside the bags, packages and boxes, and sat down on the sofa, settling Annabelle on her lap.

Kate perched on an armchair. "I don't even know where to start."

"Start with Brody. Who is he, and what's his angle?"

"What kind of a question is that? He doesn't have an angle." Kate found herself looking to the front door where Brody had left.

"I don't trust him."

"Why on earth not?"

"He came out of nowhere."

"He came from Scotland."

"And now he's here?"

"He's helping. He's been terrific, Nad. He changes diapers and everything."

"And you don't find that odd?"

"It's not odd. What are you getting at?"

Nadia lifted Annabelle so that she was standing on her lap. Annabelle reached out to grab Nadia's nose.

"You said Quentin stole from him," Nadia said.

"He did. And—I hate to say it, because it sounds terrible—I'm glad he did. If it hadn't been for that, we'd still be in LA in that horrible mansion with those awful people, and I might be fighting a losing battle to get Annabelle."

"You don't think he's ticked about that?" Nadia asked, her focus still on the baby.

"You mean ticked at Quentin?" Kate wasn't following.

"At anybody who has anything to do with Quentin."

"You mean me?" The question didn't make sense.

Brody wasn't angry with Kate. Quite the opposite. He seemed to like her a lot, quite a lot, and he'd been nothing but helpful and supportive.

"From what you've said, he's stuck to you like glue since he found out you were going for custody."

"We've been in danger. It was real."

Sympathy and concern immediately flooded Nadia's expression, and she finally looked at Kate. "I know. I'm so glad everything turned out okay."

"Thanks to Brody." Kate couldn't believe she was having to defend him.

"I'm not saying he wasn't brave."

"He stood in front of a bullet for me."

"Earning your undying trust."

Kate came to her feet. "I don't understand what you're saying. It wasn't a ploy." The idea that Brody had risked his life to get her to trust him was preposterous.

"Tell me about the lawyer," Nadia said a little more softly.

"Kalvin? I like him a lot. He's young, but he's eager. And he's got a lot of support from the senior partners. They all came to the meeting, as well."

"And Brody introduced you to him?"

Kate did a double take of her friend. "I picked him. Brody would have supported anyone I chose."

"So he made you think."

"Good grief, Nad. You've been reading way too many conspiracy theories."

"Your lawyer is from a firm that represents Shetland Tech."

"They're a very highly respected firm. They represent a lot of clients."

"But Shetland Tech and Beast Blue Designs are competitors."

"Quentin was the crook," Kate said.

"He did crooked things. Absolutely. And I'm perfectly glad he's gone. But things linger, Kate."

"Whatever you're getting at, just spit it out."

"What I'm getting at is Brody and his company, Shetland Tech, have an innate conflict of interest in helping Annabelle because she will inherit Beast Blue Designs. That conflict extends to you as her legal guardian."

Kate stilled, parsing through the statement. "He's not thinking that way."

"I can guarantee he is. Consider it, Kate. A rich Scottish royal suddenly romancing you."

"Who said he was romancing me?"

Nadia coughed out a laugh of disbelief. "The expressions on both of your faces. It's plain as day that you're sleeping with him."

Kate considered denying it, but realized it was pointless to lie. "What if I am?"

"Oh, Kate."

"Don't 'oh, Kate' me. It's a fling. He's hot. I've had flings before."

"He's staying close to you and gaining your trust to benefit his corporation."

"I don't buy that." Kate refused to believe Brody would be so callous. She moved directly to the kitchen. She was thirsty, so she opened the fridge to look for a pitcher of iced tea.

Nadia followed, carrying Annabelle. "Please, just listen, Kate. You tell him you're going for custody. He knows about Quentin's crimes, so he knows you're going to win custody of Annabelle. And suddenly, of all the women in the world that Scotland's most eligible bachelor can be with, he chooses you?"

"Thanks a lot. Want some? And what makes you say he's Scotland's most eligible bachelor?"

"You're welcome. Yes. And I did a thorough search on him, and there's a reputable magazine that officially named him Scotland's most eligible bachelor."

Kate set two tall glasses on the counter. She didn't know why she was surprised. Brody would be a great catch. He was hot, wealthy and titled to boot. He was funny and smart, and he was amazing in bed. Word might have gotten around about that.

She poured the iced tea.

"I don't like the look on your face," Nadia said.

"I don't have a look on my face."

"Where do you think this is going?"

"Nowhere. It's nothing. He's here for a few days, and then he's got some wrap-up in LA, and then he's going back to Scotland. Where he has a brother. Who is going to be the earl. And who, by the way, is probably a more eligible bachelor than Brody."

"What's he wrapping up in LA?"

"The Beast Blue thing. They need to pull all the code from 'Blue Strata Combat'."

Nadia took one of the glasses. Her tone went softer. "Which will do what?"

"Give Brody's family back their rightful property." Kate took a drink, soothing her parched throat.

"What will it do to Beast Blue Designs?"

Kate hadn't thought about that. "It'll hurt the company for sure."

"It'll destroy the company. He may bankrupt Annabelle's company."

"It's not—"

"But it is. And he doesn't know what you'll do. You might fight for Annabelle's interests. You *should* fight for Annabelle's interests. And that would be counter to Brody's interests."

Kate pulled up a stool at their small breakfast bar. "It's not like that."

But she was trying to figure out what it was like. What was Brody planning? Was he worried she'd make some kind of a move to protect Beast Blue? He didn't need to worry. She didn't have the first idea of what that move might be.

Nadia took the stool beside her. "Shetland Tech could easily bankrupt Beast Blue. They probably will, and then Annabelle will have nothing."

"Annabelle doesn't need anything." Kate reached out and took Annabelle's little hand. "She has me. She doesn't need anything else."

"But Brody doesn't know that."

"He trusts me."

"He could be hedging his bets."

Kate refused to believe Brody was being manipulative. "He stood in front of a bullet for me. You didn't see it. Rex was absolutely going to shoot him."

"Maybe," Nadia said. "If you're right, then that's

terrific, and he's an exceptional man. I'm just saying be careful. There's a lot at stake, and you're a babe in the woods."

"Your confidence in me is inspiring."

"I love you, Kate. But I've got to be honest. You need to go into this with your eyes wide-open."

"I will," Kate said.

She believed in Brody. Everything he'd done so far seemed to be for her well-being and Annabelle's. But she couldn't deny that Nadia had made some good points. Brody was a highly successful and eligible man who could have any woman in the world. Did it make any sense at all that he'd fall for Kate?

"Love the hair, by the way," Nadia said.

Kate's hand went to her short locks. Would the son of an earl honestly opt for a woman with purple hair?

Thirteen

Brody picked Kate up in his rental car, taking her to a nearby shopping mall while Annabelle napped and Nadia babysat. Kate had talked a lot about Nadia their past few days in LA. She made her friend sound intelligent, open and friendly.

That sure wasn't the vibe Brody was picking up. She seemed impatient and resentful. It was clear she loved babies, so it wasn't the introduction of Annabelle into their lives. It was equally clear she was suspicious of Brody.

She and Kate were obviously close. Maybe it was as simple as wanting to reconnect with Kate and settle into their new life without Brody around to get in the way. He had to admit, it was a reasonable thing to want.

He and Kate were strolling through the baby section of a department store. They'd picked a crib with a top safety rating, and they were now looking at blankets and something called bumper pads which apparently protected babies from the dangers of top safety rated cribs.

"I was thinking," he opened.

Kate stopped to look at a puffy blanket with an elephant pattern. "About?"

"About how long I should stay."

She turned to look at him. "Do you need to go back to Scotland? Because I wouldn't want to keep you from your family."

He wasn't wild about her enthusiasm to get rid of him. He'd hoped she'd seem at least a little bit disappointed.

"It's not about getting back to Scotland," he said.

"Oh." She didn't ask him to elaborate.

He elaborated anyway. "I don't want to overstay my welcome."

"In America? Is there a visa thing?"

"In Seattle."

She looked puzzled. "I don't think anyone cares how long you stay in Seattle."

"What about Nadia?"

Kate's expression faltered and she went back to

checking out the elephant quilt. "What does Nadia have to do with anything?"

"I bet this is a lot for her, with Annabelle coming home. I don't want to get in the way."

"What do you want?" Kate asked.

He could be honest about that. "What I want is to spend more time with you. But your feelings are more important than mine. You've been through a lot. Your life has drastically changed, and I don't want to make your life any more difficult."

At the same time, he couldn't deny he was worried about her. She'd been catapulted into a world of big money and big stakes, about to be put in de facto charge of a company that had committed a major crime.

Beast Blue had hundreds of employees. Who knew how many of them were involved, and how would she ever sort through the mess? Lawyers, accountants and technical specialists could only help so much. Ultimately, she was going to have to look after Annabelle's financial future.

"I want to help you," he said, reaching out to draw her into a loose embrace. "If you'll let me."

At first she was stiff in his arms. He chalked it up to them being in a public place. But then she relaxed and leaned into him.

"I don't want you to go yet," she said.

"Good. That's settled." He gave her a light kiss on the temple. "I'm going to miss you tonight."

She smiled. "Absence makes the heart grow fonder."

Then she seemed to realize what she'd said. Her smile disappeared, and her cheeks flushed. "I didn't mean. That is…"

"You didn't mean to make it sound romantic."

"Yes."

He knew what had her uncomfortable. It was preying on his mind, as well. They didn't know what this was, or if it was anything. And he knew they weren't in a position to figure it out.

He tried to put her at ease by lightening the mood. "I supposed it can only be so romantic here in the linens section."

She didn't smile at his joke.

"I don't know what this is either, Kate."

He truly didn't. And he was starting to wonder. His feelings for her were beyond friendship and support. But they'd been thrown together under such bizarre circumstances, and their lives couldn't be further apart. Still, he seemed to be falling fast and hard. And he couldn't begin to guess how far it would go.

"It's a fling," she said. "It's a wonderful fling, and in some respects, it's so much more. You saving my life for instance, and you proving Quentin committed a crime so that I got custody of Annabelle. That's beyond your average fling."

"No kidding."

"But the you and me part, we're just two people sleeping together for a while."

He wasn't ready to accept that. But he wasn't ready to argue it, either.

"I wish we could do that tonight," he said instead.

"I have a baby to take care of."

"You do," he agreed, knowing they weren't going to solve this here and now. "And that baby needs blankets."

Kate laughed then, and he loved the sound of it.

His phone rang in his pocket, and he checked the screen.

"Will," he told her. "Hey," he answered.

"It's a mess," said Will.

"Is that a surprise?"

"It's worse than we expected."

"In what sense?"

"They can take care of the steganography. That never made it into the mainstream programming, and we don't have a national security issue. But the Shetland Tech code is everywhere. They've used it in a dozen programs. It'll take years to pull it all apart."

Kate had moved farther down the aisle, and Brody put some additional distance between them.

"We don't have years," he said to Will.

"I've made that abundantly clear."

"Good."

"But we're going to have to bring them down, Brody. Beast Blue will cease to exist."

"So I kill Annabelle's company."

"To save your family."

"That's a terrible choice," Brody said.

"It's no choice at all."

"I suppose not."

Brody's loyalty had to be to his family. And they weren't the ones who'd committed a crime. It might not be Annabelle's fault, but it was her father's doing, and her legacy turned out to be based on theft.

"What about the mansion? Has there been any talk of Quentin's personal assets?"

"He signed personal guarantees. It'll all get eaten up in the bankruptcy proceedings."

"Everything?" Brody hated that this was how it would go.

"You might be able to make a case for Francie's personal possessions."

"The jewelry?"

"They weren't married. They didn't live together. And she didn't sign any of the personal guarantees."

"Isn't that ironic."

Quentin had tried to protect his assets from Francie, and he ended up protecting Francie's assets instead.

"You want me to pick them up from the gate-house?"

"Can you legally do that?"

"With Kate's permission, I can. But, one more thing."

Brody braced himself.

"Kate's mother will get half. Francie had some kind of old will that was written before Annabelle was born."

Brody almost laughed. "There's really no justice, is there?"

"You got justice for Shetland Tech."

"I suppose I did. I'll ask Kate."

"Let me know."

"Will do." Brody signed off and caught up to Kate.

"Everything okay?" she asked.

"It's progressing. It's going to be a long haul." He saw no reason to give her the bad news before it was concrete. "Will did have one question for you."

She gave Brody her attention. "What is it?"

"It'll make things easier if Francie's personal possessions are separated from the mansion's assets. He can pick up her jewelry if you'd like."

"You mean I'm getting the emeralds after all?"

"You are."

"Is it just me, or is that kind of funny?"

"I almost laughed. One glitch though. Your mother will get half."

Kate rolled her eyes. "Oh, good grief. They shouldn't go to either of us. They should go to Annabelle."

"I don't suppose suggesting that to your mother would help?" Brody was sure he knew the answer. The woman he'd seen in the courtroom wasn't about to give up a windfall.

"There's no point in even asking," Kate said. "She will be firmly convinced she's entitled."

"Maybe it'll keep her away." As soon as the words were out of his mouth, he rethought them. "I'm sorry. She's your mother."

"I'm not going to pretend to admire her now. Her staying away from Annabelle is the best outcome of this. If it costs us a few emeralds, so be it."

"That's the spirit."

"Now, help me with this. Elephants or bunnies?"

"The bunnies are adorable."

"I thought so, too."

He leaned down to whisper, letting his lips brush the shell of her ear. "And you're adorable."

"No," she said in a firm voice.

"No?"

"I'm not going to your hotel before we relieve Nadia. You can make it through one night on your own."

He wasn't so sure about that.

Then again, he had a lot to think about and a bunch of phone calls to make. Will was right. Brody had to protect his family's legacy.

Kate and Brody walked along the path on Sunday morning, pushing Annabelle in her new stroller. Families were picnicking, children were riding bikes, and dads and sons were playing catch. She'd never paid much attention to the activities in the park near her condo, but she realized now it was a hub of activity.

"I'm having a hard time picturing it," Kate said as she watched a little girl climb up the slide. "I mean, I can wrap my head around a baby, but I can't imagine Annabelle as a child. She'll go to school, maybe take dance lessons, or soccer or fencing. She might like fencing."

"Fencing?" Brody asked, pointing to a vacant bench.

Annabelle had fallen asleep, and now he parked the stroller, and they sat down to take in the sights.

"You never know what she might like. Whatever it is, I'll support it. I'm going to be a regular mom. I'm going to bake cookies for the bake sale, register her in swimming lessons, buy her ice cream at the zoo."

"All the things your own mother never did," Brody guessed.

"She's going to be happy," Kate said with conviction.

"You want some ice cream?" He pointed to a concession stand. "You've given me a craving."

"Sure." Kate leaned back and tipped her face up to the sunshine. She couldn't remember being this happy. "Make mine chocolate."

"You got it." Brody rose from the bench and walked across the path, weaving his way through the picnic tables. She watched him, admiring his great looks, his height and confident stride.

He placed his order and then turned back to her. He smiled and waved, and her heart took a flip. If family life in suburbia was like this, she was going to love it. Annabelle at three, at six, and nine. Brody—

Her fantasy screeched to a halt.

Brody wasn't going to be there. Brody was only hers for a short while. Soon he'd get on a plane. He'd fly off to Scotland. He'd play polo, attend fancy balls, meet glamorous women and eventually produce the next generation of little earls to live in his big, drafty castle.

But that was his life, and it made sense for him.

She and Annabelle were much better here, she told herself.

And, who knew, over time maybe Kate would meet a nice man, an accountant or an architect. She could get married and have some brothers and sisters for Annabelle.

She tried to picture her future husband, but Brody kept getting in the way. That was understandable, she told herself. Because he was walking this way, a smile on his face, two chocolate ice-cream cones in his hands.

It was impossible to plan beyond Brody. And why should she try? There was nothing wrong with enjoying this moment. She was under no illusions. She wouldn't get hurt when he left. Her heart wouldn't be broken, because she'd been prepared for the end before it had even happened.

"Chocolate all around," he said, handing her one of the cones before sitting back down beside her.

They both licked the melting edge of their ice cream.

"This is nice," Brody said, gazing around at the trees and flowers. "It's a lot like Scotland—like the cities, anyway. The countryside is wilder, more rugged."

"I've always lived in cities," she said.

"I went to university in Edinburgh, but I mostly grew up in the country."

"In a castle. I heard. You don't have to brag."

He chuckled. "Believe me, it's nothing to brag about."

"Sure, it is. What kid doesn't dream of being a prince or princess, of growing up surrounded by finery in a castle with a beautiful, kindly queen as a mother?"

"Was that your dream?" he asked.

"For a while. When I was nine." She wasn't going to lie. "I just knew I'd have a beautiful golden dress, and a little gold crown, and jeweled shoes."

"Jeweled shoes?"

"What? You don't have any jeweled shoes?"

"Since I'm not an entertainer in Vegas, no."

"Well, I would have had jeweled shoes. Like I said. When I was nine." She licked her ice cream.

"And afterwards? Or before? You obviously had other dreams."

"This," she said, scanning the scene in front of her. "This was my dream."

He smiled at that. "You're living your dream, Kate."

"At least for a little while."

He adjusted the hood on the stroller to block the sun from Annabelle. "For a long while, I think."

Kate didn't want to disagree. But her dream had included a husband. And she couldn't imagine where that might be in her future.

"What did I say?" he asked.

"Nothing." She shook off her mood.

He slid closer. "Seriously, Kate. What happened just then?"

She opened her mouth to lie. But then she caught his gaze with her own.

"I'm going to miss you." The truth came out before she could stop it.

His expression softened, his eyes going opaque. He touched his index finger to her chin. "I'm going to miss you, too."

Neither of them moved.

"How did this happen?" she asked.

"I have no idea," he said. "There I was, busy minding my own business."

"You were undercover investigating a crime."

"You were undercover saving a baby."

"One minute we were arguing," she said.

"And the next we discovered we had something in common."

"I don't want to sleep alone tonight," she said.

Brody looked concerned. "What would Nadia think?"

"It doesn't matter what Nadia thinks. I know what I think."

He gave a wry smile. "She might throw me out of the condo."

"Not if we go to your hotel."

Annabelle stirred in the stroller.

Brody's hand smoothed Kate's shoulder. "You are welcome in my hotel room anytime you want."

Fourteen

Brody awoke to Annabelle's coos. She was in a portable crib in the corner of the hotel room playing with her toes in the morning light.

He looked down at Kate sleeping beside him, and his chest contracted with emotion. She was right where she belonged. And so was he.

His phone rang, and he quickly scooped it up, hoping it wouldn't wake her.

He slipped from the bed and padded into the small living room, keeping his voice down.

"Hello?"

"It's Will."

"Morning." Brody checked out the coffeemaker to see if he could figure out how to make a pot.

"I've been up all night."

"Anything wrong?"

"No. I had an idea. Well, it was Kalvin's idea, but I agree with him."

"Okay." Brody managed to free the small coffeepot from the holder. He turned to the sink and filled it.

"Hear me out?"

"Sure."

"It's going to sound crazy."

"I'm half asleep, trying to work a hotel coffee-maker. Talk slow and use small words, and you'll probably be fine."

"Why don't you call room service?"

"Because I'm talking to you." Brody located a packet of Colombian coffee and tore it open.

"Okay, I'm going to plunge right in," Will said.

"You're not plunging very fast."

"Shetland Tech buys Beast Blue."

"What?" Brody spilled the coffee grounds. He cursed.

"You said you'd hear me out."

"I'm listening." There was another package in the service basket and he took it.

"You could get it for pennies on the dollar. It's all but worthless as it stands. If Shetland buys it, then it doesn't matter who stole what. We get our game 'Mercury Mayhem' to market first as planned.

But then we follow it up with some of Beast Blue's games, then more of ours, and we own the space."

"We compete with ourselves."

"Yes."

Brody immediately thought of one complication. "Beast Blue employees are going to be hostile. And some of them had to know about the theft. I don't want a bunch of dishonest people working for me."

He pressed the switch on the coffeemaker and stood back.

"That would have to be part of the process, yes," Will said. "We'd identify those who were involved and fire them."

"Before they could do any damage?"

"Oh, yeah. There are ways to keep people contained in a technical environment. We lock it down, and keep people out until we've vetted them."

"These are very talented programmers. You don't think they might break in and cause trouble?"

"Are you questioning my technological savvy?"

"No. I'm just a cautious man."

"Who stands in front of bad guys pointing guns," Will said.

"We're going to stop talking about that now."

"Okay, boss. But what do you think of my idea?"

The aroma of coffee filled the air. Brody inhaled and turned over a cup.

"Is it even possible to do right now?" he asked. "They're not going to let Kate make such a far-reaching decision while she's only Annabelle's temporary guardian."

"She'd have to do it in conjunction with the executor and the advocate appointed by the court."

"The court-appointed advocate has that kind of power?"

"They have a vote. Kalvin says they can do this kind of thing in cases involving minors and money."

Brody took a mental step back. "So Annabelle would get something out of this. She might do okay?"

"That all depends on you. But for her any kind of a sale is better than bankruptcy."

Brody began to get excited. He poured himself a cup of coffee, taking a first sip as he walked away from the mess. He wanted his brain to be fully functional. If this worked, it could be a win-win.

"I'll talk to Kate and call you back," he said to Will.

"If she has any questions, loop me in."

"Thanks." Brody ended the call.

He could hear Kate moving in the bedroom, her soft voice as she talked to Annabelle. Taking another sip of coffee, he moved to the doorway. He leaned his shoulder on the doorjamb, watching her.

In a fluffy hotel robe, hair mussed, feet bare, she leaned into the crib and lifted Annabelle.

"Did you have a good sleep, darling?" she asked, rubbing her nose to Annabelle's.

"Bah," Annabelle said. "Bah, bah."

"You always make your point so eloquently. Are you hungry, or would you like a change first."

"Bah, bah." Annabelle batted at her cheek.

"Change it is. Between you and me, I think that's a good decision."

Kate caught sight of Brody, and she smiled. "Morning."

"Good morning to you, pretty ladies." He moved into the room and gave Kate a kiss. Then he rubbed Annabelle's hair and stroked his thumb across her soft cheek.

He felt like a very lucky man. He wished he could stop time and stay in this moment forever.

But he knew he couldn't. Since he couldn't keep them, the best he could do was protect them. And he would. He wouldn't let his own family down, but he wouldn't throw Kate and Annabelle to the wolves, either.

"I have an idea," he said to Kate.

"For breakfast?" she asked.

"For life."

She looked startled.

"It wasn't exactly my idea. It was Will's. Well, really it was Kalvin's."

"You've been talking to my lawyer?" There was something odd in her voice when she asked the question.

"I've been talking to Will, why?"

She shrugged and her expression smoothed out. "No reason. What did Will say?"

"He said…" Brody hesitated. He didn't know why he was hesitating. This was good news.

Kate bent to the diaper bag and retrieved a diaper, the change pad and some wet wipes.

"He suggested Shetland Tech should buy Beast Blue Designs."

She looked puzzled. "You should buy it? Why would you want to buy it?"

"Two reasons, really."

Instead of looking at him, she spread the change pad out on the bed and laid Annabelle on top.

"First is, well I didn't say anything to you before now," Brody continued speaking. "Because I didn't want you to worry. But Beast Blue is in serious trouble. To stop using the Shetland code, they're going to have to dismantle most of their new games. They're going to have to pay hefty fines. And it's going to cost the company a fortune."

"You expected that, though." Kate was bent over the baby, and Brody couldn't see her face.

"I did. But it's worse than we anticipated. It'll bankrupt the company."

She looked up at that. "Would that be a good thing? For you, I mean."

"For Shetland Tech. Sure. Theoretically, losing a major competitor in the marketplace is good for Shetland."

"So, are you happy?"

He sat down on the bed to be level with her profile. "I'm not happy at the prospect of Annabelle losing all her money."

"It was Quentin's money."

"You can't be happy at the thought of losing it all."

She frowned. "I'm not my mother, Brody."

"What the heck is that supposed to mean?"

"I mean, I'm not looking for a big score. Getting Annabelle was never about the money." With one hand on Annabelle's stomach so the baby couldn't roll over, Kate shook out the new diaper.

"Nobody said it was."

"You just did."

"No, I didn't."

"You just tippy-toed up to telling me there wouldn't be any money. Clearly, you thought I'd care."

"Most people would care." He was trying to be patient here.

"Well, I don't." She deftly swooped the diaper beneath Annabelle's bottom.

"Okay. That's good. You're a better person than most."

"Thank you."

"You're welcome. And, well, this is going to seem rather anticlimactic then."

She waited.

"It's the second reason. Will and Kalvin—and I agree with them—figured out that if Shetland Tech buys Beast Blue, then we don't need to untangle their entire year's R&D. As a wholly owned company they—well, we—can use the stolen code and sell the products as they were designed."

She lifted Annabelle from the bed and straightened up. Her gaze narrowed on him. "And what does that mean?"

"It means what it sounds like. Shetland Tech pays for Beast Blue—in other words Annabelle—instead of causing the company to go completely bankrupt. Quentin signed personal guarantees. If Beast Blue goes down, the mansion and everything else is gone."

"But what does it mean for Shetland Tech?"

"That's the beauty of it. It's a win-win."

"But more a win for Shetland Tech."

"It was always going to be more of a win for Shetland Tech. We have the advantage of having not broken the law."

Annabelle started to fuss, and Kate patted her back. "And you came up with the plan with my lawyer."

"It was Kalvin's idea, yes."

"The lawyer you introduced me to." She reached into the diaper bag and produced a bottle.

"Kate, what is wrong?"

"A lawyer from a firm that just happens to represent Shetland Tech?"

"Are you accusing me of something?"

Annabelle reached for the bottle and cried out.

"What are we doing here, Brody?"

He came to his feet. "I honestly haven't the vaguest notion."

She popped the bottle into Annabelle's mouth. "If it's all the same to you, Brody, I think I'll hire my own lawyer from here on in."

"What?"

"I want a lawyer that I know is taking care of Annabelle."

"Are you saying Kalvin has a conflict of interest?"

Her gaze had gone hard. "I guess I am. This is all just a little too convenient. You and Annabelle's lawyer suddenly discover it's in her best interest to sell to you, ensuring Shetland Tech will have the market all to themselves and be wildly successful."

"You don't trust me." That surprised him. In fact it hurt him more than it surprised him. He didn't like the feeling.

"I did trust you. But Nadia had you pegged. I stood up for you. I figured any guy who'd stand in front of a bullet for me had to be honest."

"I have been nothing but honest." Even as he said the words, he knew they sounded ridiculous.

He'd lied to her from the moment he met her. But she'd lied to him, as well. And he thought they'd worked that out. He sure hadn't lied to her since.

"Right." She put Annabelle down in the crib, making sure she had a grip on the bottle. "And a rich royal from Scotland is falling for a public-school teacher who owns half a condo with a sky-high mortgage."

"You think I'm a snob?" Hell, yes he was falling for her.

She started to get dressed. "Nadia said you were playing me, that you were sticking to me to get to Annabelle. I pretended it wasn't true. I pretended that you hadn't turned on a dime when you found out I wanted guardianship."

"I turned on a dime because you needed my help."

"And because you liked me so much." Her voice

dripped with sarcasm. "And you wanted to be with me. I hope the sex wasn't too much trouble for you."

"Kate, you're losing your mind."

"No, I'm opening my eyes." She was fully dressed now, and she shoved her feet into her shoes.

"Are you leaving?" he asked. "Is that what you're doing? You're leaving?"

Brody's phone rang.

"I'm going to find Annabelle a new lawyer," she said.

"Find whatever lawyer you want." He immediately realized that would be a good thing. It would prove he was being honest with her. "That's the best thing you can do, Kate. They'll tell you I'm offering you a lifeline. I'm doing it for Annabelle."

He'd been doing it for Kate as well, but in this moment he really didn't feel like helping her.

His phone rang again.

He reached for it and saw it was Blane.

Kate lifted Annabelle from the crib.

"I have to take this," Brody said.

She paused in the doorway. "Don't let us stop you."

"Don't go."

"This was a mistake."

"I'm on your side."

"I don't believe you."

His phone rang a third time.

"Then go." He tried not to feel bitter, but he failed. "Talk to a lawyer who's never even heard my name before and see what he says. But when you come back, you better hope I'm still willing to buy the company."

She turned and walked out.

Brody answered the call. "Yeah?"

"Brody?" Blane's voice was rough.

Fear shot through Brody. "What's wrong?"

Blane had a fit of ragged coughing. "You'd better come home. Hurry."

Brody immediately headed for his suitcase. "Are you with a doctor?"

"They want to do surgery. Mother and Father are pretty upset."

"What kind of surgery? Never mind. I'll get the doctor's number from Mother. I'm on my way. You do what they tell you. Save your strength."

Brody threw his clothes into the suitcase. He shouldn't have stayed here with Kate. It was selfish. He should have gone home. Even if Blane seemed temporarily better, he should have gone home to support his brother.

Kate had spent two hours in a lawyer's office in Seattle that first day, tossing out all kinds of accusations about Brody, Shetland Technology and Kalvin.

The lawyer had then spent at least that on the phone with Kalvin. They'd called in technical experts and financial experts, and Kate had paid him nearly a month's salary.

Now, close to a week later, she'd been told, in essence, that she was a fool. Everything Brody had said to her was accurate and correct. Shetland Tech would be throwing Annabelle a lifeline by purchasing Beast Blue. Sure, it would work out okay for Brody and his family, but Shetland Tech was going to do well in any event.

For Annabelle, Beast Blue, and all of their employees, most of whom were completely innocent, Brody's offer was the only way out.

Armed with enough information to make her feel wretched, she arrived home where Nadia was babysitting Annabelle.

"Well?" Nadia asked as soon as she walked in. "What did he say?"

Kate closed the door and leaned against it. "He said Annabelle should have accepted Brody's offer. And I shouldn't have doubted him."

Nadia's expression fell. "What do you mean?"

"Brody wasn't trying to take advantage of the situation. He wasn't after anything he couldn't have gotten without ever saying a word to me, never mind saving my life and helping me with Annabelle."

Nadia dropped into the nearest chair. "Oh, Kate."

Kate dumped her purse on the floor and walked into the living room. Her legs were feeling wobbly.

"Is it my fault?" Nadia asked. "I feel like it's my fault."

"It's not your fault. You didn't know him. I did. I knew him. I slept with him. He told me about his family, his brother." She groaned and sat down on the sofa. "I should have trusted him."

"He is royalty." Nadia paused. "I'm just sayin', the mathematical odds…"

"It wasn't like he fell madly in love with me." Kate only wished that could have happened. "He was attracted to me, and he was honest with me. And anything he said or did, when he held me and kissed me, it was because he wanted to, not because he was attempting to get at Annabelle."

"Was it good?" Nadia asked. "The sex, the romance?"

"It was amazing." Kate closed her eyes and remembered. "He was so, I don't know, so everything. Sweet and funny, and wicked smart. He got my jokes. He made them better. He understood that I had to take care of Annabelle. He never questioned that. And he was good with her. He was honestly good with her."

"Uh-oh," Nadia said.

"What?" Could things get even worse?

"You fell in love with him."

"No, I didn't."

That would be bad. That would be terrible. If Kate had fallen in love with Brody, she was going to have her heart broken. She refused to have her heart broken. Not on top of everything else. Not on top of losing Brody.

Losing Brody was the worst thing that had ever happened to her.

"Oh, no," she moaned. Her hands started to tremble. "How could I have let this happen?"

"What are you going to do?"

"Do? There's nothing I can do. Don't you think I've done enough?"

"You could apologize." Nadia's suggestion was tentative.

"I should." Kate didn't disagree with that. "I owe it to him."

"But?"

"I don't think I can. I don't think I can bring myself to talk to him."

"An email?" Nadia suggested.

"That would be lame. Not to mention insulting. He was really angry that last day, Nad. And he had a right to be angry."

Kate's mind went back. "That last morning. He

looked so good. He was so happy. We slept together. We woke up with Annabelle. We'd gone to the park the day before. And then we ordered room service for dinner. That way, Annabelle could play in her crib while we ate. It was like we were this happy little family." She groaned and dropped her head into her hands.

"Uh, Kate?"

"What?"

"He would have gone back to Scotland."

Kate spread her fingers and peeked out.

"Fight or no fight, he wasn't staying in Seattle."

Kate straightened. "I know that."

"Do you? Because for a minute there it sounded like you were thinking happily ever after."

Kate tried to make herself laugh. "I didn't go that far over the edge."

"Uh-oh," Nadia said again.

"No," Kate insisted. "I had my head on straight the whole time. I know his life is over there." She stopped herself. What was she saying? Brody's life in Scotland was far from the only thing keeping them from happily ever after.

"I'm a rational person," Kate continued. "Even if his life wasn't over there, I get that I'm indulging in this fantasy all by myself. It was never his fantasy. He liked me, sure. I get that. And he wasn't conning me, which is noble. But he wasn't falling in love with me. I know that for a fact."

"Do you?" Nadia asked.

Fifteen

"Her lawyer called," Kalvin told Brody over the phone from across the Atlantic.

"We knew he would," Brody said.

It had taken a little longer than he'd hoped, but the lawyer had seen the value in Shetland Tech's offer.

"What do you want to do about the deal?" Kalvin asked.

"Let it go through."

"So, you're going to forgive her?" Blane asked from where he reclined in a lounger in the Calder Castle garden. The day was warm, and Blane was recovering quickly from the surgery on his airway.

"You're being way too generous," Kalvin said. "As your legal counsel, I have to advise you—"

"Advise away," Brody said. "But the deal stands."

It wasn't Annabelle's fault that Kate had trust issues. And it wasn't Annabelle's fault that Brody let common sense rush out the door the minute he'd laid eyes on Kate.

Annabelle hadn't chosen her parents. For that matter, she hadn't chosen her headstrong auntie, either. She was stuck with what life had dealt her. And Brody wasn't going to be the guy to take away her inheritance. He'd make sure both Annabelle and Kate could live comfortably for the rest of their lives.

"Are you making a bad deal?" Blane asked.

"I can email a scan of the paperwork," Kalvin said. "You'll need to get it notarized at your end."

"As long as she'll sign, too."

"Oh, she'll sign. I set that lawyer of hers straight on a few things."

Brody chuckled. "You shouldn't have such a thin skin."

"He initially threatened to bring me up on charges with the bar."

"You didn't do anything wrong."

"I know. And now he knows it, too."

"And Kate knows it?"

"She sure does."

Brody had half hoped for an apology from her. She'd made some wild accusations, and she'd been dead wrong about his motives. Now that she knew it for sure, you'd think the woman could pick up the phone and admit it.

She hadn't.

And his only conclusion was that she didn't want to speak to him. She was taking the money and putting the rest behind her. He didn't know what all that intimacy and sex was about, but clearly it didn't mean nearly as much to her as it had meant to him.

"It won't bring her back to you," Blane said.

Brody shot him a glare.

"Fax the paperwork," he said to Kalvin.

"It'll be there in the morning. Goodbye, sir."

"Goodbye, Kalvin."

"That's what you really want," Blane said.

"That's not why I did it." Brody didn't bother denying that he'd wish Kate would call.

"By 'did it' you mean overpay for a company we don't really need in the first place?"

"It's going to make us a lot of money." Brody wasn't going to accept the premise that he'd overpaid. He'd paid well, but he hadn't paid more than he expected to make on the deal.

"Since you saved us from ruin, I'm going to give you this one."

"Thank you so much. Since I'm the guy running the business end of this family, I'll do whatever I bloody well please."

Blane chuckled. But then his chuckle turned into a cough.

Brody sat up straighter, regretting his outburst.

"I'm fine," Blane wheezed.

"You sure?" Brody was poised to run for Blane's nurse.

The coughing subsided. "I hate this."

"I know." Brody felt enormous sympathy for his brother.

The surgery had been a success, and a new medication had stabilized Blane's lungs.

"You know, at this rate you're going to be Earl," Blane said, recovering his breath and sitting back.

"I have no intention of ever being Earl."

"I may or may not outlive Father, but eventually, I'm going to die."

"Eventually is a long, long time," Brody said.

"I'm not getting married."

"You can't possibly know that." Brody refused to let Blane give up on having a family.

He knew his brother wanted children. And Brody wanted that for him. He also wanted it to be Blane's son to take over as Earl after Blane died as a very old man. And in the meantime, Brody wanted to live his own life.

"I'll probably live for a while," Blane said.

"You'll live for a very long time. You have to, if

only because I couldn't stand all those ceremonial events. I've got businesses to run."

"And women to chase."

"I'm done with that for a while." Brody couldn't imagine who might follow Kate. He had no interest in anyone else, and he couldn't see that changing in the short term.

"You need to get married," Blane said. "This family needs a backup plan."

"Stop that. I'm serious. I'll get married. Eventually. But you need to go first."

"Maybe." Blane smiled smugly to himself. "Now tell me again about her purple hair."

"How did Kate get back into this conversation?"

"We're talking about you getting married."

"We're talking about *you* getting married. Where have you been the past week? Or did the anesthetic permanently addle your brain?"

"My brain's not addled. You're the one who's addled."

"I'm not marrying Kate."

Even if their relationship hadn't completely broken down, she'd made it clear: her perfect life was in suburbia. Her perfect life was being a soccer and bake-sale mom for Annabelle. It was an admirable goal, but it didn't include Brody.

"You'd better marry her," Blane said.

"Why had I better?"

"Because you're in love with her."

Brody wasn't rising to the bait. "I was infatuated with her. I'm over it."

"You're the worst liar in the world."

"You didn't see me in California. I rocked at lying."

Brody had surprised himself with his acting ability.

"Maybe," Blane said. "But you suck at lying to yourself."

"I'm not lying. I'm accepting reality."

Kate was in Brody's past. There was nothing he could do to change that. He might miss her, and he might desperately wish he could be with her again. But reality was reality.

Blane wouldn't be deterred. "Give me one good reason you can't have her."

"I'll give you three. She doesn't trust me. She won't leave Seattle. And she has purple hair."

"Give me one that matters."

"Those all matter."

"No, they don't," said Blane. He counted off on his fingers. "She now knows she can trust you."

"On this, maybe. But what about the next thing?"

"Her hair will grow out. And Seattle's just geography."

"What does that even mean?"

"It means there are other places in the world to be a responsible, caring parent and raise a wonderful child. Right here, for example."

"You want me to bring Kate here?"

"That would be traditional."

"Well… I…" Brody abandoned his answer. There was no point in trying to talk sense to Blane right now. "You want something that matters?" he asked instead.

"I do."

"Okay."

Brody's brain conjured up a kaleidoscope of Kate, laughing beside the pool, dancing in his arms, pushing the stroller through the park and holding Annabelle on that last morning before he'd blown it with her.

"Brody?" Blane interrupted. "You're not saying anything."

"Here's the reason." Brody forced himself to be brutally honest. "I should never have fallen in love with her in the first place."

"I think you just made my point for me," Blane said softly.

"Yeah." Brody felt a giant weight had just settled onto his chest.

He loved Kate. He loved her more than life. Sitting here pretending he didn't was hopeless. It wasn't going to work, and his feelings weren't going to go away.

That left him with a stark choice. Live the rest of his life missing her and wondering what they might have had together. Or put his heart on his sleeve and go back to her. Maybe he was the one who should apologize.

He had to do something. He didn't want to keep living like this.

"I have to go get her," he said mostly to himself.

"You have to go get her."

"What if she says no? What if she won't consider Scotland?"

"Maybe you stay with her."

"In Seattle?"

"I don't know. All I know is that you don't give it up. If she's everything you say she is, you don't give it up."

Brody looked over his shoulder at the family castle. Could he give this up?

"It's just geography," said Blane.

Brody pictured Kate and Annabelle, and the little condo in Seattle. He pictured himself there, and it looked good.

In an instant, he knew he could give up the drafty castle. He could give up anything for Kate.

"You promise you'll get married and have a few sons?" he asked Blane. "Because if I do this, we're going to need a few more Calders."

"Deal. But I might need your help finding a willing woman."

"Oh, get over yourself. As soon as you're up and around, there'll be a lineup halfway to the village."

Kate didn't think it was possible for her to feel worse. But she was wrong. She did feel worse.

Her lawyer put the contracts in front of her, all approved and signed by the executor of Quentin's estate and the court-appointed advocate for Annabelle. As soon as Kate signed, it would be a done deal.

Brody would own Beast Blue, and Annabelle would have a portfolio of investments that would give her the means to do anything she wanted in life. Kate could do anything she wanted as well, because the allowance for raising Annabelle was ridiculously generous.

Trouble was the only thing she truly wanted was the thing she couldn't have.

"Something wrong?" the lawyer asked.

"Nothing." Kate put the pen to the line on the last page and signed.

Wild thoughts rolled through her mind on the drive home, memories and regrets. Where had she gone wrong? What should she have done differently? Would it have changed anything if she had?

She had no way of knowing what Brody thought of her now. He might well be completely over their fling. He might not have given her another thought. He might have made the deal for Beast Blue solely because it suited him. It didn't mean he cared about her at all.

By the time she got home, she was no closer to an answer than she'd been when she started. She pulled into the short driveway and gripped the steering wheel. She had limited choices here, but she did have a couple of them. She could leave things as they were and move on with life. Or she could try to do the right thing. She could at least take a stab at doing the right thing, and maybe clear her conscience.

She stepped out of the car and slammed the door behind her. Her principles told her she needed to apologize. It was the same set of principles that had made her go after Annabelle in the first place, the same ones that had ended up putting their lives in jeopardy and lost her Brody.

"Sometimes you win. Sometimes you lose." But she knew deep down she had to stick with her beliefs.

She swung her purse over her shoulder and

marched up the walkway. One thing was sure, without principles, she had nothing.

She opened the front door to find Nadia on the floor with Annabelle, a stack of blocks between them.

"I'm doing it," she said.

"Then I'm with you," Nadia said looking up. "What exactly are we talking about?"

"I'm apologizing to Brody. I signed the contracts. Annabelle's future is secure. But I was wrong. And I'm sorry. And I'm going to tell him so."

"You're calling him?"

Annabelle knocked the colorful block tower over with a clatter. She grinned up at Kate.

"Well done, sweetheart," Kate said. "I'm not calling him."

"Emailing? That's probably better. You might get tripped up trying to talk. If you write it, you can take your time, compose it just right. And you won't have to—"

"I'm going to Scotland."

It took Nadia a moment to speak. "Say again?"

"I'm going to Scotland. I'm not wimping out on this. I'm going to face him, look him in the eye and tell him I was wrong and I'm sorry."

Nadia came to her feet. "That's a bad idea."

"It's the right thing to do."

"No, honey. It's a bad thing to do. You're sorry. I know you are. But that's not why you're going to Scotland."

"Yes, it is." Kate had just gone over this in her mind in minute detail. She knew what was right and what was wrong.

"You're going to Scotland to see if he's in love with you."

"I'm not. He's not. I'm over that fantasy."

"I know you so well, Kate. I can tell you're not over that fantasy. And I'm worried about you. If you go to him, and it's not what you hope, you're going to get your heart stomped on. And it's going to happen in person, overseas, and you'll be all by yourself when it does."

"That's not why I'm going." Was it? "I have no expectations."

Nadia put an arm around her shoulders. "Your expectations are written all over your face."

"But—"

"But, nothing. You're going to lay your heart on the line, and there's a better than even chance it's going to go completely wrong."

Kate didn't want to hear this. She did not want to hear that her last hope was gone.

"But, what do I do?"

"I tell you what you do." Nadia paused for a long time.

"What?" Kate all but shouted.

"You take me with you."

Kate swallowed against a sob, but then Nadia's words registered. "What?"

"I'm your best friend. No way I'm letting you go through this alone."

Kate couldn't help a watery smile.

"Remember when I had to stand up to that awful principal and you stuck with me till the end?"

Kate remembered.

"You should do this, Kate. If you love him that much, and it's obvious to me that you do, then it's worth the risk. For you and for Annabelle. Whatever happens, I'll be there to cheer you on and have your back."

"You'd come to Scotland?"

"I'll buy the tickets."

The Calder butler Jeremy Clive entered the library where Brody and Blane were drinking brandy. Blane was getting better in leaps and bounds. His color was back. His energy was increasing. And he claimed he felt better than he had in years.

"Sir?" Jeremy said.

"Yes?" Brody and Blane answered simultaneously.

"Sorry to disturb you, but there's a young lady in the main foyer. She declined to give her name."

Brody reached out and rapped Blane heartily on the shoulder. "You see that? Word's gotten around already."

"She's here to see you, Mr. Brody."

"Me?"

"Yes."

"How young?"

The stately Jeremy looked confused. "I would guess in her twenties. She's not a child."

"Pretty?" asked Blane.

"I would say so."

"If you don't want her, I'll take her," Blane said.

They were on their second brandy, and Blane's tolerance for alcohol seemed to have diminished while he was sick.

Brody rose to his feet. "I'll get back to you on that."

As he exited the library, he tried to figure out who might be stopping by. Jeremy knew most of his friends, and he certainly knew the people in the village, better than Brody did in fact.

He'd met a woman in the airport a couple of weeks ago. So, she was a possibility. What was her name? Mandy or Sandy or maybe Katrina? If he couldn't remember by the time he got to the entrance foyer, this was going to be a bit embarrassing.

He came around the corner of the hall and halted.

Her back was to him, and her hair wasn't purple, but he could swear it was Kate.

He blinked his eyes and gave his head a shake.

Then Annabelle's little head popped up over her shoulder, and joy surged through him. He quickly set down his drink and strode forward.

"Kate?"

She turned, and he drank in her beautiful face. Her makeup was subtle, her hair had grown longer. She'd either cut off or colored the purple bits. She was wearing a fitted, smoke-blue dress with a navy cardigan.

She looked classic and beautiful beneath the portraits and shields that decorated the hall. She looked as if she'd been born to the castle.

"You're in Scotland," he said.

"Hello, Brody."

She looked and sounded so formal, he was afraid to hug her. He stopped a foot away.

He smiled. "Hi there, Annabelle. She's grown since I saw her."

"Every day," Kate said.

"Come in." He motioned. "I'm surprised to see you."

"I hope it's okay."

"It's more than okay."

"And who do we have here?" asked Blane, making an appearance in the hall.

"This is my brother, Blane," Brody said to Kate.

She gave Blane a broad smile. It was the smile Brody wanted for himself. He felt a shaft of jealousy and an urge to shove Blane back into the library.

"Hi, Blane," she said.

"This is Kate Dunhern."

Blane's eyes went wide. "This is Kate?"

"Yes." Brody instantly worried about the brandy consumption and what it might do to Blane's judgment.

Blane strode right over to her and took her hand. "And this must be Annabelle."

"Brody mentioned us?" Kate asked.

The question set Brody back. Did she think he wouldn't? Did she think he'd tell his family the story of Quentin and LA and leave her and Annabelle out?

"He more than mentioned you," Blane said.

"That's enough," Brody interjected, fearing what might come next.

"He's in love with you."

Both Kate and Brody went completely still.

Then Brody found his voice. "Are you kidding me?" he said to Blane. He could have socked his brother.

Instead, he took Kate's hand. "Ignore him. Let's go inside." He led her away from Blane, back down the hall where he shut them into the library.

"I'm so sorry about that. He's been sick."

"I know."

"He's a little drunk right now." Brody was mortified and scrambling for the right words. "And, well, he made some funny assumptions about things I said when I first got back."

"You don't have to explain."

"He was way out of line."

She moved closer. "You don't have to explain. I came to say I'm sorry, Brody."

"For what?"

She gave him a look of disbelief. "For not trusting you. For that last morning in Seattle when I accused you of plotting against me. For throwing out everything we had together because I couldn't bring myself to—"

"Stop." He put his fingertips across her lips.

"You won't accept my apology?" She looked positively demoralized.

He stepped closer.

"Gah," Annabelle told him softly. She reached out and patted his lips.

"Gah," he said in return. "Kate, you don't owe me an apology," he said.

"Yes, I do." He shook his head. "I behaved terribly, and you made the deal anyway. You took care of Annabelle, and of me."

"I love you." He couldn't hold it in any longer. "My brother is right. I love you, Kate."

She blinked at him, seeming completely flustered. "I don't even know what that means."

"It means I love you." It felt good to say it over and over.

"But... What..."

"I think the 'what' depends on you."

She still looked confused.

"Do you love me back?"

"Yes," she answered quickly. "Oh, yes." Then she gave a nervous laugh. "I guess I should have said that right away, shouldn't have I?"

"It's traditional."

"I meant, what does that mean for us? You live here and I live there, and..."

He smiled. He almost laughed. "What do you want it to mean?"

"You keep answering my questions with questions."

"That's because I don't care about anything but loving you. We can do anything. We can live anywhere. It'll have to be together. But beyond that, I'm open."

She looked around the room. "Hmmm. Well. This is a big castle."

"It is that."

"My condo's pretty small."

"No argument from me. But Seattle has other houses, bigger houses. And I understand you've recently come into some money."

"You'd do that for us? You'd move?"

"I'd do that."

This time when she smiled, her eyes shimmered with tears.

"I'm going to kiss you now," he said. "We can finish this conversation later. But right now I'm going to kiss you."

"Oh, please do." She raised her lips to his.

Epilogue

In the anteroom of the cathedral, Brody double-checked his tie. His gray vest was smooth under the crisp tuxedo jacket, and his cuff links bore the Calder family crest. He wanted to look perfect, not that anyone would be looking at him. All attention would be focused squarely on Kate.

The heavy oak door to the chapel hallway swung open, and he turned, expecting to see Blane checking on his parents.

Instead, it was Kate rushing into the room in a cloud of tulle and lace.

"You can't be here," he told her, quickly averting his eyes. It took about three seconds for curiosity to get the best of him, and he glanced up.

She looked wonderful, classy and elegant in a satin

and jeweled snow-white gown. Lace decorated her smooth shoulders, the bodice was fitted to her slim waist, while the filmy, full skirt cascaded out from a satin belt.

"I'm not supposed to see you in that." Even as he said the words, he continued to stare at her.

Her hair was a soft cloud around her beautiful face, dark lashes emphasizing her brilliant blue eyes. And her lips looked dark and luscious. He couldn't wait for the part where he got to kiss her.

"I have an idea," she said, her voice bright and excited.

"Now? You're risking bad luck on our wedding day to bring me an idea?"

She swept closer. "With all we've been through, we're stronger than bad luck."

Coming closer still, she held out her hand to reveal a coin in her palm.

"Is the limo parked at a meter?" he joked.

"I've been thinking," she said. "We shouldn't get married without knowing where we're going to live."

The pressure was obviously getting to her. "You want to talk about which country to live in ten minutes before the ceremony?"

"Heads," she said, "we live in Scotland. Tails we live in Seattle."

"I can't keep up with you. What're you saying?"

"Or..." A mischievous twinkle came into her eyes.

"We could buy a vacation home in the San Juan Islands."

"Is that in the Caribbean?"

"They're off the coast of Washington State, close to Seattle."

"A vacation home in Washington State? Is this some kind of a wedding present?"

Her grin went wide.

"Kate, sweetheart, are you saying what I think you're saying?" He felt like he'd won the lottery for a second time this year.

"We should stay in Scotland, Brody. I want to raise our family right here."

He wanted to pull her into his arms and hold her tight. But he didn't dare. She looked so perfect, he couldn't let himself muss her up.

"Okay with you?" she asked, looking suddenly uncertain.

"It's more than okay with me. You know my parents will be completely thrilled."

"I know." She took his hands. "Your mother and I talked last night. I know this is really important to your family."

He gave her hands a squeeze. "What's important here is us, you and me. You don't have to commit right now."

"I want to commit right now."

"Are you completely sure about this?"

"I'm completely sure, Brody. I thought about it all night."

"When my mother starts being 'the Countess' she can be formidable."

"I know she can. But she didn't intimidate me. It's what I want."

"In that case I couldn't be happier. Thank you, Kate." He hesitated for a split second, but then decided to share his own secret. "And… Well… Speaking of mothers…"

Kate sobered. It only took her a second to glean his meaning. "Brody, I told you, you can't call her."

"I know you told me that. But, well, you weren't going to call her." He sure hoped he hadn't made a mistake here.

"We were leaving well enough alone. She was happy about getting half of Francie's jewelry. Do you know how hard it is to make her happy? You don't mess with it once it happens. You don't need to put a target on your back."

"I didn't call her."

Kate looked relieved.

"I flew her here."

Kate's jaw dropped. "Here, as in Scotland?"

"Here, as in the cathedral."

Kate's hand went to her forehead. "Why would you do that?"

Brody held her other hand fast. "You can't get married without your mother. It's not right. She's your only family."

He reached out to touch the chickadee charm on her necklace. In Annabelle, Francie was still there with them, too. He was grateful to Francie. He always would be.

"I'm not worried about me," Kate said. "I can handle my mother. It's you. You're rich. You're royalty. She's going to latch onto you like—"

"I've taken care of that."

"Oh, really. You've taken care of my mother, have you?

Brody checked his watch. They only had about two minutes left to talk.

"I bought her a little condo in Santa Monica."

Kate's jaw dropped open.

"It's in a seniors complex. And they have people there to help her, keep an eye on her really."

"You didn't."

"I did."

Kate started to speak, but then her expression turned relieved and joyous.

She gave her head a bemused shake. "Okay. But you're a wonderful man. I think she's going to like it very much."

"I don't want you to have to worry about her."

"I won't worry. With you around, I've stopped having anything to worry about."

"Good."

"But I better go be a bride now."

"You better go be a bride. But one more thing." Brody wanted her to go into the ceremony on a purely happy note.

"Is it bad?"

"No, it's good. Christina is here, too."

Kate's face broke into a wide smile over that one. "You brought Christina all the way to Scotland for our wedding?"

"I did, but not just for the wedding."

"She's on vacation?"

"I hired her. She's staying to help with Annabelle."

"Do we need a nanny?"

"Well, you've got one whether you want one or not."

He could tell from her expression that she was warming to the idea.

"I don't know what you want to do," he told her. "Work or help my mother with charities, or be a full-time mom to Annabelle and all the other babies that come along. But you can have help to do it. I want you to have help to do it."

"Annabelle loves Christina."

"I know. And Christina is excited to be here."

"Brody?"

"Yes?"

"You can kiss the bride."

"I'm not going to wreck your pretty makeup." But he wanted to kiss her. He desperately wanted to kiss her.

He settled for a quick peck on her cheek.

Just then Blane arrived in the doorway.

He instantly zeroed in on Kate.

He gave her a mock scowl. "How did you get in here?"

"Through the door," she answered jauntily.

From minute one, she hadn't been the least bit intimidated by his brother the viscount. Brody couldn't help musing that Blane needed to find a woman like Kate. Not Kate, of course, never Kate.

"Out you go," he ordered, pointing to the door. "You have to know better than to let him see you before the ceremony."

"We're immune to bad luck," Kate said.

"Well, nobody's immune to Father Callum. Get back where you belong."

Kate grinned unrepentantly. "See you in five minutes," she said to Brody. "And your kissing better have improved by then."

Blane snickered as Kate left.

"Inside joke," Brody said.

"Uh-huh."

"I kiss just fine."

"I hope so. You're not going to hold on to a woman like that with lame kisses."

"She's not going anywhere."

"You sure?" There was a familiar teasing twinkle in Blane's eyes. Brody felt like they were kids again.

"In four minutes, she'll be mine for life. I'm grateful. I never thought I'd find someone so special." Brody meant every word.

"Let's go, brother." Blane clapped him on the back. "You've got a bride to marry."

Brody and Blane entered the chapel from a side door and made their way in front of the altar.

The church was completely filled with friends, relatives, a few London royals and people from the town. Blake met his mother's gaze in the front row. She was beaming. Sitting next to her, even his father looked proud. The earl was an aloof and exacting man. It wasn't often that Blane or Brody pleased him.

Then the piper's music rose, and Nadia appeared at the end of the aisle. She was carrying Annabelle, who was dressed in an opulent mauve gown. It set off Nadia's sophisticated royal purple.

"You've inspired me, brother," Blane muttered.

Brody rose a curious brow in Blane's direction.

"If you can find someone as wonderful as Kate, then it's time I went for it, too."

Brody found himself grinning with approval. "Good for you."

"I hear couples first meet at wedding receptions all the time."

"They do?"

"See that woman in row five? In the bright green dress?"

"She's pretty."

"I'm dancing with her first. If it doesn't work out, I'll try the redhead in row eight, left side, on the aisle."

Brody had to stifle a laugh.

Then the processional music came up, and Kate appeared. Brody had already seen her, but he was taken all over again by the beautiful dress, a heather bouquet from his highlands, the classic Calder diamond tiara and her serene smile that was all for him. The congregation gasped with her beauty.

She was stunning.

With every step that brought Kate closer to him, his heart filled with love and joy.

When she finally arrived, she handed Nadia her bouquet and gave Annabelle a kiss. Then she looked into Brody's eyes, hers filled with unconditional love. They joined hands, and he didn't look away until the vows were finished.

Then he kissed her properly. The congregation grew restless at the length, but he didn't care. When he drew away, she was well and truly his wife.

He took Annabelle from Nadia, and held her in his arms. Then he took Kate's hand to walk back down the aisle.

"Nice kiss," she whispered breathlessly, hanging on to his arm.

"I do aim to please."

"Your mother," she said.

"You want to talk about my mother right now?"

"I thought you should know. When we talked, she also said she expects us to get pregnant tonight."

Brody nudged Kate gently as they smiled to the people they passed. "Did you tell her we'd already taken care of that little thing?"

"I did not. I think we can save that announcement for another day."

"Good." He wasn't yet ready to share their secret.

Then the double doors opened in front of them. The bells pealed. A crowd on the grounds outside cheered loudly. And Brody introduced his family to his world.

* * * * *